THREE TALES OF

MY FATHER'S DRAGON

MY FATHER'S DRAGON
ELMER AND THE DRAGON
THE DRAGONS OF BLUELAND

By **RUTH STILES GANNETT**
Illustrated by **RUTH CHRISMAN GANNETT**

Random House 🏠 New York

http://www.randomhouse.com/

Library of Congress Cataloging–in–Publication Data
Gannett, Ruth Stiles. Three tales of my father's dragon / by Ruth Stiles Gannett ;
illustrated by Ruth Chrisman Gannett. p. cm. Contents: My father's dragon — Elmer and the dragon —
The dragons of Blueland. Summary: A compilation of three tales which relate the fantastic adventures
of Elmer Elevator and a baby flying dragon named Boris.
ISBN 0-679-88911-6 (trade). — ISBN 0-679-98911-0 (lib. bdg.)
[1. Dragons—Fiction.] I. Gannett, Ruth Chrisman, ill. II. Title. PZ7.G15Th 1998 [Fic]—dc21 97–25215

Printed in the United States of America 10 9 8 7 6 5 4

CONTENTS

A Note from the Author

When I wrote it, I had no idea that my story about Elmer and his dragon would become such a success. *My Father's Dragon* was written to amuse myself while between jobs. I wrote it for fun, with no expectation of publication. What a happy surprise it was when Random House accepted it!

Turning my story into a book was a family project. My stepmother was chosen to do the illustrations, and my husband-to-be chose the type. It was a happy collaboration. And when the book appeared in 1948, it promptly won an award—it became a Newbery Honor Book.

The second and third stories, *Elmer and the Dragon* and *The Dragons of Blueland*, came along a few years later. These stories were harder to write than the first one. *My Father's Dragon* had seemed to write itself and I wasn't sure if I could write a sequel, but I did, twice. Since then, my dragon stories have been translated into eight languages and have been read by children all over the world.

Through the years, readers have asked for a fourth story, even offering plots to consider. I have thanked them but declined, while encouraging them to write their own. For myself, I prefer to leave Elmer and Boris and his family safe at home.

Ruth Stiles Gannett

For My
FATHER

MY FATHER'S DRAGON

Chapter One

MY FATHER MEETS THE CAT

One cold rainy day when my father was a little boy, he met an old alley cat on his street. The cat was very drippy and uncomfortable so my father said, "Wouldn't you like to come home with me?"

This surprised the cat—she had never before met anyone who cared about old alley cats—but she said, "I'd be very much obliged if I could sit by a warm furnace, and perhaps have a saucer of milk."

"We have a very nice furnace to sit by," said my father, "and I'm sure my mother has an extra saucer of milk."

My father and the cat became good friends but my father's mother was very upset about the cat. She hated

cats, particularly ugly old alley cats. "Elmer Elevator,"
she said to my father, "if you think I'm going to give

that cat a saucer of milk, you're very wrong. Once you start feeding stray alley cats you might as well expect to feed every stray in town, and I am *not* going to do it!"

This made my father very sad, and he apologized to the cat because his mother had been so rude. He told the cat to stay anyway, and that somehow he would bring her a saucer of milk each day. My father fed the cat for three weeks, but one day his mother found the cat's saucer in the cellar and she was extremely angry. She whipped my father and threw the cat out the door, but later on my father sneaked out and found the cat. Together they went for a walk in the park and tried to think of nice things to talk about. My father said, "When I grow up I'm going to have an airplane. Wouldn't it be wonderful to fly just anywhere you might think of!"

"Would you like to fly very, very much?" asked the cat.

"I certainly would. I'd do anything if I could fly."

"Well," said the cat, "if you'd really like to fly that much, I think I know of a sort of a way you might get to fly while you're still a little boy."

"You mean you know where I could get an airplane?"

"Well, not exactly an airplane, but something even better. As you can see, I'm an old cat now, but in my younger days I was quite a traveler. My traveling days are over but last spring I took just one more trip and sailed to the Island of Tangerina, stopping at the port of Cranberry. Well, it just so happened that I missed the boat, and while waiting for the next I thought I'd look around a bit. I was particularly interested in a place called Wild Island, which we had passed on our way to Tangerina. Wild Island and Tangerina are joined together by a long string of rocks, but people never go to Wild Island because it's mostly jungle and inhabited by very wild animals. So I decided to go across the rocks and explore it for myself. It certainly is an interesting place, but I saw something there that made me want to weep."

WILD ISLAND

RIVER

Chapter Two

MY FATHER RUNS AWAY

"Wild Island is practically cut in two by a very wide and muddy river," continued the cat. "This river begins near one end of the island and flows into the ocean at the other. Now the animals there are very lazy, and they used to hate having to go all the way around the beginning of this river to get to the other side of the island. It made visiting inconvenient and mail deliveries slow, particularly during the Christmas rush. Crocodiles could have carried passengers and mail across the river, but crocodiles are very moody, and not the least bit dependable, and are always looking for something to eat. They don't care if the animals have to walk around the river, so that's just what the animals did for many years."

"But what does all this have to do with airplanes?" asked my father, who thought the cat was taking an awfully long time to explain.

"Be patient, Elmer," said the cat, and she went on with the story. "One day about four months before I arrived on Wild Island a baby dragon fell from a low-flying cloud onto the bank of the river. He was too young to fly very well, and besides, he had bruised one wing quite badly, so he couldn't get back to his cloud. The animals found him soon afterwards and everybody said, 'Why, this is just exactly what we've needed

all these years!' They tied a big rope around his neck and waited for the wing to get well. This was going to end all their crossing-the-river troubles."

"I've never seen a dragon," said my father. "Did you see him? How big is he?"

"Oh, yes, indeed I saw the dragon. In fact, we became great friends," said the cat. "I used to hide in the bushes and talk to him when nobody was around. He's not a very big dragon, about the size of a large black bear, although I imagine he's grown quite a bit since I left. He's got a long tail and yellow and blue stripes. His horn and eyes and the bottoms of his feet are bright red, and he has gold-colored wings."

"Oh, how wonderful!" said my father. "What did the animals do with him when his wing got well?"

"They started training him to carry passengers, and even though he is just a baby dragon, they work him all day and all night too sometimes. They make him carry loads that are much too heavy, and if he complains, they twist his wings and beat him. He's always tied to a stake on a rope just long enough to go across the river. His only friends are the crocodiles, who say 'Hello' to him once a week if they don't forget. Really, he's the most miserable animal I've ever come across. When I left I promised I'd try to help him someday, although I couldn't see how. The rope around his neck is about the biggest, toughest rope you can imagine, with so many knots it would take days to untie them all.

"Anyway, when you were talking about airplanes, you gave me a good idea. Now, I'm quite sure that if you were able to rescue the dragon, which wouldn't be the least bit easy, he'd let you ride him most anywhere, provided you were nice to him, of course. How about trying it?"

"Oh, I'd love to," said my father, and he was so angry at his mother for being rude to the cat that he didn't feel the least bit sad about running away from home for a while.

That very afternoon my father and the cat went down to the docks to see about ships going to the Island of Tangerina. They found out that a ship would be sailing the next week, so right away they started planning for the rescue of the dragon. The cat was a great help in suggesting things for my father to take with him, and she told him everything she knew about Wild Island. Of course, she was too old to go along.

Everything had to be kept very secret, so when they found or bought anything to take on the trip they hid it behind a rock in the park. The night before my father sailed he borrowed his father's knapsack and he and the cat packed everything very carefully. He took chewing gum, two dozen pink lollipops, a package of rubber bands, black rubber boots, a compass, a tooth-brush and a tube of tooth paste, six magnifying glasses, a very sharp jackknife, a comb and a hairbrush, seven hair ribbons of different colors, an empty grain bag with a label saying "Cranberry," some clean clothes, and enough food to last my father while he was on the ship. He couldn't live on mice, so he took twenty-five peanut butter and jelly sandwiches and six apples, be-cause that's all the apples he could find in the pantry.

When everything was packed my father and the cat went down to the docks to the ship. A night watchman was on duty, so while the cat made loud queer noises to distract his attention, my father ran over the gangplank onto the ship. He went down into the hold and hid among some bags of wheat. The ship sailed early the next morning.

Chapter Three

MY FATHER FINDS THE ISLAND

My father hid in the hold for six days and nights. Twice he was nearly caught when the ship stopped to take on more cargo. But at last he heard a sailor say that the next port would be Cranberry and that they'd be unloading the wheat there. My father knew that the sailors would send him home if they caught him, so he looked in his knapsack and took out a rubber band and the empty grain bag with the label saying "Cranberry." At the last moment my father got inside the bag, knapsack and all, folded the top of the bag inside, and put the rubber band around the top. He didn't look just exactly like the other bags but it was the best he could do.

Soon the sailors came to unload. They lowered a big net into the hold and began moving the bags of wheat. Suddenly one sailor yelled, "Great Scott! This is the queerest bag of wheat I've ever seen! It's all lumpy-like, but the label says it's to go to Cranberry."

The other sailors looked at the bag too, and my father, who was in the bag, of course, tried even harder to look like a bag of wheat. Then another sailor felt the bag and he just happened to get hold of my father's elbow. "I know what this is," he said. "This is a bag of dried corn on the cob," and he dumped my father into the big net along with the bags of wheat.

This all happened in the late afternoon, so late that the merchant in Cranberry who had ordered the wheat didn't count his bags until the next morning. (He was a very punctual man, and never late for dinner.) The sailors told the captain, and the captain wrote down on a piece of paper, that they had delivered one hundred and sixty bags of wheat and one bag of dried corn on the cob. They left the piece of paper for the merchant and sailed away that evening.

My father heard later that the merchant spent the whole next day counting and recounting the bags and feeling each one trying to find the bag of dried corn on the cob. He never found it because as soon as it was dark my father climbed out of the bag, folded it up and put it back in his knapsack. He walked along the shore to a nice sandy place and lay down to sleep.

My father was very hungry when he woke up the next morning. Just as he was looking to see if he had anything left to eat, something hit him on the head. It was a tangerine. He had been sleeping right under a tree full of big, fat tangerines. And then he remembered that this was the Island of Tangerina. Tangerine trees grew wild everywhere. My father picked as many as he had room for, which was thirty-one, and started off to find Wild Island.

He walked and walked and walked along the shore, looking for the rocks that joined the two islands. He walked all day, and once when he met a fisherman and asked him about Wild Island, the fisherman began to shake and couldn't talk for a long while. It scared him that much, just thinking about it. Finally he said, "Many people have tried to explore Wild Island, but not one has come back alive. We think they were eaten by the wild animals." This didn't bother my father. He kept walking and slept on the beach again that night.

It was beautifully clear the next day, and way down the shore my father could see a long line of rocks leading out into the ocean, and way, way out at the end he could just see a tiny patch of green. He quickly ate seven tangerines and started down the beach.

It was almost dark when he came to the rocks, but there, way out in the ocean, was the patch of green. He sat down and rested a while, remembering that the cat had said, "If you can, go out to the island at night, because then the wild animals won't see you coming along the rocks and you can hide when you get there." So my father picked seven more tangerines, put on his black rubber boots, and waited for dark.

It was a very black night and my father could hardly see the rocks ahead of him. Sometimes they were quite high and sometimes the waves almost covered them, and they were slippery and hard to walk on. Sometimes the rocks were far apart and my father had to get a running start and leap from one to the next.

After a while he began to hear a rumbling noise. It grew louder and louder as he got nearer to the island. At last it seemed as if he was right on top of the noise, and he was. He had jumped from a rock onto the back of a small whale who was fast asleep and cuddled up between two rocks. The whale was snoring and making more noise than a steam shovel, so it never heard

my father say, "Oh, I didn't know that was you!" And it never knew my father had jumped on its back by mistake.

For seven hours my father climbed and slipped and leapt from rock to rock, but while it was still dark he finally reached the very last rock and stepped off onto Wild Island.

Chapter Four

MY FATHER FINDS THE RIVER

The jungle began just beyond a narrow strip of beach; thick, dark, damp, scary jungle. My father hardly knew where to go, so he crawled under a wahoo bush to think, and ate eight tangerines. The first thing to do, he decided, was to find the river, because the dragon was tied somewhere along its bank. Then he thought, "If the river flows into the ocean, I ought to be able to find it quite easily if I just walk along the beach far enough." So my father walked until the sun rose and he was quite far from the Ocean Rocks. It was dangerous to stay near them because they might be guarded in the daytime. He found a clump of tall grass and sat down. Then he took off his rubber boots and ate three more tangerines. He could have eaten twelve but he hadn't seen any tangerines on this island and he could not risk running out of something to eat.

My father slept all that day and only woke up late in the afternoon when he heard a funny little voice saying, "Queer, queer, what a dear little dock! I mean, dear, dear, what a queer little rock!" My father saw a tiny paw rubbing itself on his knapsack. He lay very still and the mouse, for it *was* a mouse, hurried away muttering to itself, "I must smell tumduddy. I mean, I must tell somebody."

My father waited a few minutes and then started down the beach because it was almost dark now, and he was afraid the mouse really would tell somebody. He walked all night and two scary things happened. First, he just had to sneeze, so he did, and somebody close by said, "Is that you, Monkey?" My father said, "Yes." Then the voice said, "You must have something on your back, Monkey," and my father said "Yes," because he did. He had his knapsack on his back. "What do you have on your back, Monkey?" asked the voice.

My father didn't know what to say because what would a monkey have on its back, and how would it sound telling someone about it if it did have something? Just then another voice said, "I bet you're taking your sick grandmother to the doctor's." My father said "Yes" and hurried on. Quite by accident he found out later that he had been talking to a pair of tortoises.

The second thing that happened was that he nearly walked right between two wild boars who were talking

in low solemn whispers. When he first saw the dark shapes he thought they were boulders. Just in time he heard one of them say, "There are three signs of a recent invasion. First, fresh tangerine peels were found under the wahoo bush near the Ocean Rocks. Second, a mouse reported an extraordinary rock some distance from the Ocean Rocks which upon further investigation simply wasn't there. However, more fresh tangerine peels were found in the same spot, which is the third sign of invasion. Since tangerines do not grow on our island, somebody must have brought them across the Ocean Rocks from the other island, which may, or may not, have something to do with the appearance and/or disappearance of the extraordinary rock reported by the mouse."

After a long silence the other boar said, "You know, I think we're taking all this too seriously. Those peels probably floated over here all by themselves, and you know how unreliable mice are. Besides, if there had been an invasion, *I* would have seen it!"

"Perhaps you're right," said the first boar. "Shall we retire?" Whereupon they both trundled back into the jungle.

Well, that taught my father a lesson, and after that he saved all his tangerine peels. He walked all night and toward morning came to the river. Then his troubles really began.

Chapter Five

MY FATHER MEETS SOME TIGERS

The river was very wide and muddy, and the jungle was very gloomy and dense. The trees grew close to each other, and what room there was between them was taken up by great high ferns with sticky leaves. My father hated to leave the beach, but he decided to start along the river bank where at least the jungle wasn't quite so thick. He ate three tangerines, making sure to keep all the peels this time, and put on his rubber boots.

My father tried to follow the river bank but it was very swampy, and as he went farther the swamp became deeper. When it was almost as deep as his boot tops he got stuck in the oozy, mucky mud. My father tugged and tugged, and nearly pulled his boots right off, but at last he managed to wade to a drier place. Here the jungle was so thick that he could hardly see where the river was. He unpacked his compass and figured out the direction he should walk in order to stay near the river. But he didn't know that the river made a very sharp curve away from him just a little way beyond, and so as he walked straight ahead he was getting farther and farther away from the river.

It was very hard to walk in the jungle. The sticky leaves of the ferns caught at my father's hair, and he kept tripping over roots and rotten logs. Sometimes the trees were clumped so closely together that he couldn't squeeze between them and had to walk a long way around.

He began to hear whispery noises, but he couldn't see any animals anywhere. The deeper into the jungle he went the surer he was that something was following him, and then he thought he heard whispery noises on both sides of him as well as behind. He tried to run, but he tripped over more roots, and the noises only came nearer. Once or twice he thought he heard something laughing at him.

At last he came out into a clearing and ran right into the middle of it so that he could see anything that might try to attack him. Was he surprised when he looked and saw fourteen green eyes coming out of the jungle all around the clearing, and when the green eyes turned into seven tigers! The tigers walked around him in a big circle, looking hungrier all the time, and then they sat down and began to talk.

"I suppose you thought we didn't know you were trespassing in our jungle!"

Then the next tiger spoke. "I suppose you're going to say you didn't know it was our jungle!"

"Did you know that not one explorer has ever left this island alive?" said the third tiger.

My father thought of the cat and knew this wasn't true. But of course he had too much sense to say so. One doesn't contradict a hungry tiger.

The tigers went on talking in turn. "You're our first little boy, you know. I'm curious to know if you're especially tender."

"Maybe you think we have regular meal-times, but we don't. We just eat whenever we're feeling hungry," said the fifth tiger.

"And we're very hungry right now. In fact, I can hardly wait," said the sixth.

"I *can't* wait!" said the seventh tiger.

And then all the tigers said together in a loud roar, "Let's begin right now!" and they moved in closer.

My father looked at those seven hungry tigers, and then he had an idea. He quickly opened his knapsack and took out the chewing gum. The cat had told him that tigers were especially fond of chewing gum, which was very scarce on the island. So he threw them each a piece but they only growled, "As fond as we are of chewing gum, we're sure we'd like you even better!" and they moved so close that he could feel them breathing on his face.

"But this is very special chewing gum," said my father. "If you keep on chewing it long enough it will turn green, and then if you plant it, it will grow more chewing gum, and the sooner you start chewing the sooner you'll have more."

The tigers said, "Why, you don't say! Isn't that fine!" And as each one wanted to be the first to plant the chewing gum, they all unwrapped their pieces and began chewing as hard as they could. Every once in a while one tiger would look into another's mouth and say, "Nope, it's not done yet," until finally they were all so busy looking into each other's mouths to make sure that no one was getting ahead that they forgot all about my father.

Chapter Six

MY FATHER MEETS A RHINOCEROS

My father soon found a trail leading away from the clearing. All sorts of animals might be using it too, but he decided to follow the trail no matter what he met because it might lead to the dragon. He kept a sharp lookout in front and behind and went on.

Just as he was feeling quite safe, he came around a curve right behind the two wild boars. One of them was saying to the other, "Did you know that the tortoises thought they saw Monkey carrying his sick grandmother to the doctor's last night? But Monkey's grandmother died a week ago, so they must have seen something else. I wonder what it was."

"I told you that there was an invasion afoot," said

the other boar, "and I intend to find out what it is. I simply can't stand invasions."

"Nee meither," said a tiny little voice. "I mean, me neither," and my father knew that the mouse was there, too.

"Well," said the first boar, "you search the trail up this way to the dragon. I'll go back down the other way through the big clearing, and we'll send Mouse to watch the Ocean Rocks in case the invasion should

decide to go away before we find it."

My father hid behind a mahogany tree just in time, and the first boar walked right past him. My father waited for the other boar to get a head start on him, but he didn't wait very long because he knew that when the first boar saw the tigers chewing gum in the clearing, he'd be even more suspicious.

Soon the trail crossed a little brook and my father, who by this time was very thirsty, stopped to get a drink of water. He still had on his rubber boots, so he waded into a little pool of water and was stooping down when something quite sharp picked him up by the seat of the pants and shook him very hard.

"Don't you know that's my private weeping pool?" said a deep angry voice.

My father couldn't see who was talking because he was hanging in the air right over the pool, but he said, "Oh, no, I'm so sorry. I didn't know that everybody had a private weeping pool."

"Everybody doesn't!" said the angry voice, "but I do because I have such a big thing to weep about, and I drown everybody I find using my weeping pool." With that the animal tossed my father up and down over the water.

"What—is it—that—you—weep about—so much?" asked my father, trying to get his breath, and he thought over all the things he had in his pack.

"Oh, I have many things to weep about, but the biggest thing is the color of my tusk." My father squirmed every which way trying to see the tusk, but it was through the seat of his pants where he couldn't possibly see it. "When I was a young rhinoceros, my tusk was pearly white," said the animal (and then my father knew that he was hanging by the seat of his pants from a rhinoceros' tusk!), "but it has turned a nasty yellow-gray in my old age, and I find it very ugly. You see, everything else about me is ugly, but when I had a beautiful tusk I didn't worry so much about the rest.

Now that my tusk is ugly too, I can't sleep nights just thinking about how completely ugly I am, and I weep all the time. But why should I be telling you these things? I caught you using my pool and now I'm going to drown you."

"Oh, wait a minute, Rhinoceros," said my father. "I have some things that will make your tusk all white and beautiful again. Just let me down and I'll give them to you."

The rhinoceros said, "You do? I can hardly believe it! Why, I'm so excited!" He put my father down and danced around in a circle while my father got out the tube of tooth paste and the toothbrush.

"Now," said my father, "just move your tusk a little nearer, please, and I'll show you how to begin." My father wet the brush in the pool, squeezed on a dab of tooth paste, and scrubbed very hard in one tiny spot. Then he told the rhinoceros to wash it off, and when the pool was calm again, he told the rhinoceros to look in the water and see how white the little spot was. It was hard to see in the dim light of the jungle, but sure enough, the spot shone pearly white, just like new. The rhinoceros was so pleased that he grabbed the toothbrush and began scrubbing violently, forgetting all about my father.

Just then my father heard hoofsteps and he jumped behind the rhinoceros. It was the boar coming back from the big clearing where the tigers were chewing gum. The boar looked at the rhinoceros, and at the toothbrush, and at the tube of tooth paste, and then he scratched his ear on a tree. "Tell me, Rhinoceros," he said, "where did you get that fine tube of tooth paste and that toothbrush?"

"Too busy!" said the rhinoceros, and he went on brushing as hard as he could.

The boar sniffed angrily and trotted down the trail toward the dragon, muttering to himself, "Very suspicious—tigers too busy chewing gum, Rhinoceros too

busy brushing his tusk—must get hold of that invasion.
Don't like it one bit, not one bit! It's upsetting everybody terribly—wonder what it's doing here, anyway."

Chapter Seven

MY FATHER MEETS A LION

My father waved goodbye to the rhinoceros, who was much too busy to notice, got a drink farther down the brook, and waded back to the trail. He hadn't gone very far when he heard an angry animal roaring,

"Ding blast it! I told you not to go blackberrying yesterday. Won't you ever learn? What will your mother say!"

My father crept along and peered into a small clearing just ahead. A lion was prancing about clawing at his mane, which was all snarled and full of blackberry twigs. The more he clawed the worse it became and the madder he grew and the more he yelled at himself, because it was himself he was yelling at all the time.

My father could see that the trail went through the clearing, so he decided to crawl around the edge in the underbrush and not disturb the lion.

He crawled and crawled, and the yelling grew louder and louder. Just as he was about to reach the trail on the other side the yelling suddenly stopped. My father looked around and saw the lion glaring at him. The lion charged and skidded to a stop a few inches away.

"Who are you?" the lion yelled at my father.

"My name is Elmer Elevator."

"Where do you think you are going?"

"I'm going home," said my father.

"That's what you think!" said the lion. "Ordinarily I'd save you for afternoon tea, but I happen to be upset enough and hungry enough to eat you right now." And he picked up my father in his front paws to feel how fat he was.

My father said, "Oh, please, Lion, before you eat me, tell me why you are so particularly upset today."

"It's my mane," said the lion, as he was figuring how many bites a little boy would make. "You see what a dreadful mess it is, and I don't seem to be able to do anything about it. My mother is coming over on the dragon this afternoon, and if she sees me this way I'm afraid she'll stop my allowance. She can't stand messy manes! But I'm going to eat you now, so it won't make any difference to you."

"Oh, wait a minute," said my father, "and I'll give you just the things you need to make your mane all tidy and beautiful. I have them here in my pack."

"You do?" said the lion. "Well, give them to me, and perhaps I'll save you for afternoon tea after all," and he put my father down on the ground.

My father opened the pack and took out the comb and the brush and the seven hair ribbons of different colors. "Look," he said, "I'll show you what to do on your forelock, where you can watch me. First you brush a while, and then you comb, and then you brush again until all the twigs and snarls are gone. Then you divide it up in three and braid it like this and tie a ribbon around the end."

As my father was doing this, the lion watched very carefully and began to look much happier. When my father tied on the ribbon he was all smiles. "Oh, that's wonderful, really wonderful!" said the lion. "Let me have the comb and brush and see if I can do it." So my

father gave him the comb and brush and the lion
began busily grooming his mane. As a matter of fact,
he was so busy that he didn't even know when my
father left.

Chapter Eight

MY FATHER MEETS A GORILLA

My father was very hungry so he sat down under a baby banyan tree on the side of the trail and ate four tangerines. He wanted to eat eight or ten, but he had only thirteen left and it might be a long time before he could get more. He packed away all the peels and was about to get up when he heard the familiar voices of the boars.

"I wouldn't have believed it if I hadn't seen them with my own eyes, but wait and see for yourself. All the tigers are sitting around chewing gum to beat the band. Old Rhinoceros is so busy brushing his tusk that he doesn't even look around to see who's going by, and they're all so busy they won't even talk to me!"

"Horsefeathers!" said the other boar, now very close to my father. "They'll talk to me! I'm going to get to the bottom of this if it's the last thing I do!"

The voices passed my father and went around a curve, and he hurried on because he knew how much more upset the boars would be when they saw the lion's mane tied up in hair ribbons.

Before long my father came to a crossroads and he stopped to read the signs. Straight ahead an arrow pointed to the Beginning of the River; to the left, the Ocean Rocks; and to the right, to the Dragon

Ferry. My father was reading all these signs when he heard pawsteps and ducked behind the signpost. A beautiful lioness paraded past and turned down toward the clearings. Although she could have seen my father if she had bothered to glance at the post,

she was much too occupied looking dignified to see anything but the tip of her own nose. It was the lion's mother, of course, and that, thought my father, must mean that the dragon was on this side of the river. He hurried on but it was farther away than he had judged. He finally came to the river bank in the late afternoon and looked all around, but there was no dragon anywhere in sight. He must have gone back to the other side.

My father sat down under the palm tree and was trying to have a good idea when something big and black and hairy jumped out of the tree and landed with a loud crash at his feet.

"Well?" said a huge voice.

"Well what?" said my father, for which he was very sorry when he looked up and discovered he was talking to an enormous and very fierce gorilla.

"Well, explain yourself," said the gorilla. "I'll give you till ten to tell me your name, business, your age,

and what's in that pack," and he began counting to ten as fast as he could.

My father didn't even have time to say "Elmer Elevator, explorer" before the gorilla interrupted, "Too slow! I'll twist your arms the way I twist that dragon's wings, and then we'll see if you can't hurry up a bit." He grabbed my father's arms, one in each fist, and was just about to twist them when he suddenly let go and began scratching his chest with both hands.

"Blast those fleas!" he raged. "They won't give you a moment's peace, and the worst of it is that you can't even get a good look at them. Rosie! Rhoda! Rachel! Ruthie! Ruby! Roberta! Come here and get rid of this flea on my chest. It's driving me crazy!"

Six little monkeys tumbled out of the palm tree, dashed to the gorilla, and began combing the hair on his chest.

"Well," said the gorilla, "it's still there!"

"We're looking, we're looking," said the six little

monkeys, "but they're awfully hard to see, you know."

"I know," said the gorilla, "but hurry. I've got work to do," and he winked at my father.

"Oh, Gorilla," said my father, "in my knapsack I have six magnifying glasses. They'd be just the thing for hunting fleas." My father unpacked them and gave one to Rosie, one to Rhoda, one to Rachel, one to Ruthie, one to Ruby, and one to Roberta.

"Why, they're miraculous!" said the six little monkeys. "It's easy to see the fleas now, only there are hundreds of them!" And they went on hunting frantically.

A moment later many more monkeys appeared out of a near-by clump of mangroves and began crowding around to get a look at the fleas through the magnifying glasses. They completely surrounded the gorilla, and he could not see my father nor did he remember to twist his arms.

Chapter Nine

MY FATHER MAKES A BRIDGE

My father walked back and forth along the bank trying to think of some way to cross the river. He found a high flagpole with a rope going over to the other side. The rope went through a loop at the top of the pole and then down the pole and around a large crank. A sign on the crank said:

TO SUMMON DRAGON, YANK THE CRANK
REPORT DISORDERLY CONDUCT
TO GORILLA

From what the cat had told my father, he knew that the other end of the rope was tied around the dragon's neck, and he felt sorrier than ever for the poor dragon. If he were on this side, the gorilla would twist his wings until it hurt so much that he'd have to fly to the other side. If he were on the other side, the gorilla would crank the rope until the dragon would either choke to death or fly back to this side. What a life for a baby dragon!

My father knew that if he called to the dragon to come across the river, the gorilla would surely hear him, so he thought about climbing the pole and going across the rope. The pole was very high, and even if he could get to the top without being seen he'd have to go all the way across hand over hand. The river was very muddy, and all sorts of unfriendly things might live in it, but my father could think of no other way to get across. He was about to start up the pole when, despite all the noise the monkeys were making, he heard a loud splash behind him. He looked all around in the water but it was dusk now, and he couldn't see anything there.

"It's me, Crocodile," said a voice to the left. "The

water's lovely, and I have such a craving for something sweet. Won't you come in for a swim?"

A pale moon came out from behind the clouds and my father could see where the voice was coming from. The crocodile's head was just peeping out of the water.

"Oh, no thank you," said my father. "I never swim after sundown, but I do have something sweet to offer you. Perhaps you'd like a lollipop, and perhaps you have friends who would like lollipops, too?"

"Lollipops!" said the crocodile. "Why, that is a treat! How about it, boys?"

A whole chorus of voices shouted, "Hurrah! Lollipops!" and my father counted as many as seventeen crocodiles with their heads just peeping out of the water.

"That's fine," said my father as he got out the two dozen pink lollipops and the rubber bands. "I'll stick one here in the bank. Lollipops last longer if you keep them out of the water, you know. Now, one of you can have this one."

The crocodile who had first spoken swam up and tasted it. "Delicious, mighty delicious!" he said.

"Now if you don't mind," said my father, "I'll just walk along your back and fasten another lollipop to

the tip of your tail with a rubber band. You don't mind, do you?"

"Oh no, not in the least," said the crocodile.

"Can you get your tail out of the water just a bit?" asked my father.

"Yes, of course," said the crocodile, and he lifted up his tail. Then my father ran along his back and fastened another lollipop with a rubber band.

"Who's next?" said my father, and a second crocodile swam up and began sucking on that lollipop.

"Now, you gentlemen can save a lot of time if you just line up across the river," said my father, "and I'll be along to give you each a lollipop."

So the crocodiles lined up right across the river with their tails in the air, waiting for my father to fasten on the rest of the lollipops. The tail of the seventeenth crocodile just reached the other bank.

Chapter Ten

MY FATHER FINDS THE DRAGON

When my father was crossing the back of the fifteenth crocodile with two more lollipops to go, the noise of the monkeys suddenly stopped, and he could hear a much bigger noise getting louder every second. Then he could hear seven furious tigers and one raging rhinoceros and two seething lions and one ranting gorilla along with countless screeching monkeys, led by two extremely irate wild boars, all yelling, "It's a trick! It's a trick! There's an invasion and it must be after our dragon. Kill it! Kill it!" The whole crowd stampeded down to the bank.

As my father was fixing the seventeenth lollipop for the last crocodile he heard a wild boar scream,

"Look, it came this way! It's over there now, see! The crocodiles made a bridge for it," and just as my father leapt onto the other bank one of the wild boars jumped onto the back of the first crocodile. My father didn't have a moment to spare.

By now the dragon realized that my father was coming to rescue him. He ran out of the bushes and

jumped up and down yelling, "Here I am! I'm right here! Can you see me? Hurry, the boar is coming over on the crocodiles, too. They're all coming over! Oh, please hurry, hurry!" The noise was simply terrific.

My father ran up to the dragon, and took out his very sharp jackknife. "Steady, old boy, steady. We'll make it. Just stand still," he told the dragon as he began to saw through the big rope.

By this time both boars, all seven tigers, the two lions, the rhinoceros, and the gorilla, along with the countless screeching monkeys, were all on their way across the crocodiles and there was still a lot of rope to cut through.

"Oh, hurry," the dragon kept saying, and my father again told him to stand still.

"If I don't think I can make it," said my father, "we'll fly over to the other side of the river and I can finish cutting the rope there."

Suddenly the screaming grew louder and madder and my father thought the animals must have crossed the river. He looked around, and saw something which surprised and delighted him. Partly because he had finished his lollipop, and partly because, as I told you before, crocodiles are very moody and not the least bit dependable and are always looking for something to eat, the first crocodile had turned away from the bank and started swimming down the river. The second crocodile hadn't finished yet, so he followed right after the first, still sucking his lollipop. All the rest did the same thing, one right after the other, until they were all swimming away in a line. The two wild boars, the seven tigers, the rhinoceros, the two lions, the gorilla, along with the countless screeching monkeys, were all riding down the middle of the river on the train of crocodiles sucking pink lollipops, and all yelling and screaming and getting their feet wet.

My father and the dragon laughed themselves weak because it was such a silly sight. As soon as they had recovered, my father finished cutting the rope and the dragon raced around in circles and tried to turn a somersault. He was the most excited baby dragon that ever lived. My father was in a hurry to fly away, and when the dragon finally calmed down a bit my father climbed up onto his back.

"All aboard!" said the dragon. "Where shall we go?"

"We'll spend the night on the beach, and tomorrow we'll start on the long journey home. So, it's off to the shores of Tangerina!" shouted my father as the dragon soared above the dark jungle and the muddy river and all the animals bellowing at them and all the crocodiles licking pink lollipops and grinning wide grins. After all, what did the crocodiles care about a way to cross the river, and what a fine feast they were carrying on their backs!

As my father and the dragon passed over the Ocean Rocks they heard a tiny excited voice scream, "Bum cack! Bum cack! We dreed our nagon! I mean, we need our dragon!"

But my father and the dragon knew that nothing in the world would ever make them go back to Wild Island.

THE END

For MICHAEL
and PETER

ELMER AND THE DRAGON

Chapter One

TANGERINA

Into the evening sky flew Elmer Elevator aboard the gentle baby dragon, leaving Wild Island behind forever. Elmer, who was nine years old, had just rescued the dragon from the ferocious animals who lived on the island. An old alley cat told him how the dragon had been hurt when he fell from a cloud onto the island, and how the wild animals had made him their miserable prisoner. Elmer, feeling sorry for the dragon, and also hoping to fly on his back, had set off to the rescue.

Now the dragon was free, and happy and grateful, and he said, "Elmer, you were wonderful to come all the way to Wild Island just to rescue me. I'll never be able to thank you enough!"

"Oh, that's all right," said Elmer. "Flying on your back makes all my trouble worthwhile."

"Then I'll take you on a trip! Where would you like to go?"

"Everywhere," said Elmer. "The trouble is that I ran away ten days ago to rescue you, and I guess I ought to be getting home."

"Well, at least I can fly you there."

"That would be swell," said Elmer, peering over the dragon's side. "Let's rest tonight down there on Tangerina Island, and start the trip tomorrow."

"Fine," said the dragon, swooping down and landing beneath a tree on the beach of Tangerina.

Elmer slid down and took off his knapsack. "You're beautiful!" he said, admiring the dragon's blue and yellow stripes, his red horn and eyes, his great long tail, and especially his gold-colored wings shining in the faint moonlight.

"It's very kind of you to say so," said the dragon, suddenly feeling very hungry. "What's there to eat around here?"

"Tangerines all over the place!" said Elmer, picking one and peeling it for the dragon.

"Pew! Pew! What a terrible taste!" choked the dragon, spitting out the tangerine as hard as he could.

"What do dragons eat?" asked Elmer.

"I used to enjoy the skunk cabbages and the ostrich ferns on Wild Island, but I don't see any here," said the dragon, looking anxiously up and down the empty beach.

"Maybe you'd like the tangerine peelings?" suggested Elmer.

The dragon closed his eyes and carefully bit off a small corner of a piece of a peel. Then he jumped up yelling, "Why, they're delicious!"

So Elmer and the dragon ate nineteen tangerines, Elmer the insides and the dragon the peels. A chilly wind blew along the beach and the dragon curled his great long tail around the boy to keep him warm. "Good night!" said Elmer, resting his head on his knapsack. "I can't wait for the trip home tomorrow."

Next morning, as the sun edged over the horizon, the dragon rubbed his eyes, stretched his wings, and yawned. "My, but it's good to be free again! By the way, Elmer, where do you live?"

"In Nevergreen City near Evergreen Park on the coast of Popsicornia," mumbled Elmer, who was already awake and eating tangerines.

"I hope you know how to get there," said the dragon.

"Don't you?" asked Elmer.

"No, don't you?" asked the dragon.

"No," said Elmer. "You see, I came here in the bottom of a boat and I couldn't see where I was going."

"The seagulls will know," said the dragon. "They

follow ships out to sea."

"I'll go ask one," said Elmer, suddenly remembering that it would be nice to be home for his father's birthday. He walked down to the water where a very old gull was blinking at the morning sun.

"Excuse me," said Elmer, "but did you ever hear of Nevergreen City?"

"Of course," croaked the very old gull. "I lived there before I followed a ship to Tangerina, but I wouldn't dream of going back now."

"That's very interesting," said Elmer, "but would you know how to go if you did want to?"

"Certainly!" answered the old gull, pointing his right wing toward the ocean. "Just fly in exactly that direction until you get there."

Elmer took out his compass and found that this direction was west northwest. "Is it very far?"

"Far? I should say so!"

"Well, thanks a lot," said Elmer.

"I'm kind of worried," said the dragon. "Suppose we never find it?"

"We'll find it, all right," said Elmer, who was a tiny bit worried himself.

The dragon ran along the beach warming up his wings while Elmer packed sixty-nine tangerines, as many as his knapsack would hold. Besides the tangerines, he had in his knapsack all sorts of things left over from the rescue, including seven pink lollipops (which he was saving for an emergency), half a pack-

age of rubber bands, three sticks of chewing gum, a
very good jackknife, and a burlap bag. Of course, he
kept his compass in his pocket where it would be
handy, and he wore his black rubber boots.

"Are you ready?" asked Elmer.

"Jump on!" said the dragon.

Elmer clambered onto the dragon's back and took
one last look at Tangerina and the blue and white
waves skipping in from the cold ocean onto the
sandy beach.

Chapter Two

STORM

They flew all morning, high above the endless blue and white waves. Elmer sat feeling the wind on his face, listening to the whir of the dragon's wings, and watching the compass to make sure they were going in the right direction.

"I see a rock down there," said the dragon in the late afternoon. "Let's rest a bit."

"Good idea," said Elmer.

The dragon circled down to the rock, landing on all four feet. Elmer unpacked eleven tangerines and as he and the dragon ate they watched the sky turn from blue to gray and then to dark gray.

"Looks like a storm," said Elmer.

"Yes," said the dragon. "Do you think we'd better wait here or go on?"

"If the wind's bad, the waves will wash right over this rock," said Elmer. "But if we keep going maybe we can fly away from the storm."

"Let's hurry on," said the dragon, and up they flew while the waves grew whiter and wilder.

"I felt a drop of rain," said Elmer, looking up at the blackening sky.

Suddenly a ferocious wind rushed up from behind, pushing them forward faster and faster. Thunder crackled all around them, and cold hard rain beat down upon them.

"I wish I had my raincoat," yelled Elmer.

"I wish it weren't raining!" panted the dragon. "My wings are getting heavy and I can't fly very well. Besides, I hate thunder!"

The wind blew harder and the rain was colder. Elmer looked at his compass and cried through the

rumbling storm, "We're going in the wrong direction!"

"I can't help it. The wind's too strong. I can't fight against it," screamed the dragon.

Elmer put away his compass and looked down at the thrashing spray. He could hear the dragon breathing hard, and he watched his wings beating slower and slower. He wondered how long the tired dragon could fly through the crashing storm.

"I can't go on," puffed the dragon, and he sank through the rain nearer to the cold wild water. Elmer shut his eyes and held on as hard as he could, trying not to cry or think about home.

"I'm sorry," huffed the dragon, "that I couldn't keep my promise."

"Oh, that's all right. You did your best," sobbed Elmer.

And then the dragon sank lower, closer to the water. Splash!

"Elmer, we're safe! I landed on sand!" yelled the dragon. "But don't get off, because the water is up to my knees."

Elmer opened his eyes and looked around, but it was too dark to see anything. "Are you very uncomfortable?" he screamed above the noise of the storm.

"It's not too bad," shrieked the dragon, "but I think

the water's getting deeper."

"Gosh, maybe you're sinking in quicksand!"

"No, I don't think so. Anyway, where else can I go? We'll just have to wait here. Why don't you take a nap? I can sleep standing up, you know."

"A nap in the middle of the ocean in the middle of a storm?"

"Why not? There's nothing else to do."

So Elmer lay down along the dragon's back and they both were so tired that they fell asleep while the thunder boomed all around them.

"Elmer! Elmer! My stomach's under water," cried the dragon, suddenly waking up an hour later.

Elmer looked around. The storm was nearly over, but all he could see was drizzly rain and the water lapping against the dragon's stomach. "Poor dragon, would you like a pink lollipop?" asked Elmer, deciding that this was a real emergency.

"I'd rather have a cup of hot milkweed milk, but I

guess a lollipop would help," said the dragon.

Elmer unpacked one for himself and one for the dragon, and then carefully crawled along the dragon's neck until he could put the lollipop into his mouth.

"It does help a little," shivered the dragon.

As they were sucking their pink lollipops in the middle of the ocean, the drizzly rain turned into thick, thick fog and then the water began to get shallower.

"My stomach's out of water again," announced the dragon cheerfully.

"I know why the water goes up and down!" exclaimed Elmer. "It's the tide, and we're on a sand bar near some land, and just as soon as the fog lifts we'll be able to see what kind of land it is!"

"I hope it's dry land," said the dragon.

All night the water got shallower and shallower, and Elmer and the dragon were too excited to sleep. Finally, as the sun rose, even the dragon's feet were out of water, and the fog began to rise.

Chapter Three

THE SAND BAR

The fog rolled along the sand bar and out over the water and suddenly Elmer shouted, "There, behind you! Look at the pretty little green island!"

"But Elmer, I can't! I can't move. Oh, Elmer, I hurt all over." The dragon grunted and groaned and strained and struggled but he was too stiff to move at all. "Elmer, do you really see dry land, not far off?"

"Nice near dry green land, and the water's shallow all the way. Are you sure you can't move?"

"I'll try again. How stupid! I can't even see the land after waiting here for it all night long in the soaking wet water," complained the dragon, glaring at the miles of ocean before him, which was all he could see.

Elmer walked around to the dragon's head and pretended not to notice that he was crying.

"Elmer, I guess I'm not much of a dragon. A little storm comes along and forces me down, and I stand in a little water for a little while and it makes me so stiff that I can't move a single muscle."

"That's not at all true," said Elmer. "It was a big storm, and you stood in a lot of cold water for a very long time, and besides, you're only a baby dragon and you're not used to flying long distances. And just as soon as the sun dries you off, you'll be unstiff again. Have another lollipop."

"Thanks, Elmer."

"But you'd better get unstiff pretty quick because the tide will come in and you'll be up to your stomach in water again."

"No, no," whimpered the dragon.

"Well, I'll hang on your neck and see if it will bend," suggested Elmer. He jumped up and caught

the dragon's neck. He dangled for a moment and then
both he and the neck thumped down on the sand.

"Ouch!" groaned Elmer and the dragon.

"Now, can you see the island between your legs?"

The dragon carefully curled his head under to
look, and then he shouted, "I see it now, Elmer! It's
really there. What a lovely little dry island! Now help
me limber up my right front leg."

Elmer pulled very hard on the dragon's right front
leg until it would bend. Then he worked on the left

back leg, and the left front leg, and the right back leg, and started all over again with the right front leg. At last the dragon could turn around and walk. By now it was hot, and steam rose up all along the dragon's back as the sun beat down on his water-soaked wings.

Elmer started for the island and the dragon hobbled slowly behind. They went along the sand bar as far as they could and then waded into the shallow water. Elmer was still wearing his black rubber boots, but the dragon muttered, "I hate oceans!" as he splashed along stiff-leggedly.

Finally they came to the pebbly beach of the tiny island. Above them rose a cliff, and green vines hung over the edge, making a pool of shade. Elmer and the dragon sat down and ate fifteen tangerines, leaving forty-three more in the knapsack. "I wonder who lives on this island," said Elmer, wiping his mouth on his sleeve. "I think that's a path over there. Come on, let's go exploring."

"I'm afraid I'll have to rest a while longer," said the dragon. "My wings are still wet and heavy, and I'm awfully hungry. Tangerine peels don't really fill me up, and I'm terribly thirsty, and maybe I'm going to faint."

"Then you rest here in the shade while I go to look for food and water," said Elmer as he picked up his knapsack and went off to follow the little path.

Chapter Four

THE ISLAND

The path wound between boulders on the beach and then rose steeply through a crack in the cliff. Elmer scrambled up, bracing himself between the rock walls until he could find the next toehold. Just as he thought he could go no farther he found an old log ladder going straight up to the top of the cliff. "Somebody must live here," he thought as he climbed up the last rung and sat down. All around him rose beautiful tall pine trees standing in rows, and he said, "Trees don't grow in rows all by themselves. These pines were planted here by somebody a long time ago."

Elmer ate four more tangerines, and then started through the pines to look for food and water. At last he came out onto a sloping meadow. He saw a brook winding its way down the slope and he ran to take a long cool drink.

"The dragon will be happy to see this," he thought. "But I do wish I'd find somebody to tell us where we are and how to get home." He followed the brook up the slope into an old, old apple orchard. Some of the trees had rotted down to stumps, but they had been planted in rows, too. Elmer didn't see anybody anywhere, so he followed the brook back down the slope to a place where it made a pool of clear, cold water. He stooped down for another drink and found an old wooden bucket carved out of the trunk of a tree. "This bucket hasn't been used for many years," he thought as he scraped off the moss and weeds. "Maybe nobody lives here anymore."

Elmer left the bucket beside the pool and followed the brook through ferns and bushes until it turned into a swamp. "Skunk cabbages and ostrich ferns all over the place!" yelled Elmer, who was worried about the hungry, thirsty baby dragon. He quickly pulled up six skunk cabbages and ran back through the bushes to the pool. He dipped the bucket half full, threw in the cabbages, and hurried through the meadow to the pines and the dragon.

He knew he couldn't go down the ladder with the bucket, so he crawled to the edge of the cliff and peered through the vines. There was the wilted baby dragon, snoring in the shade.

"Dragon! Dragon! Wake up! I've got water and skunk cabbages for you!"

The dragon slowly opened one eye and looked up at Elmer. Then he quickly opened the other and said, "Where?"

"Right here in a bucket. But I can't bring it down to you. You'll have to let me pour the water down your throat. Ready?"

"Ready," said the dragon, tipping back his head.

Elmer aimed and poured and the dragon drank. Then Elmer threw down the cabbages one by one, and the dragon caught each cabbage in the air, laughing and crying at the same time because he was so happy and hungry and thirsty.

"That's all," said Elmer, "but there's lots more up on the island, and ostrich ferns, too. Can you fly up now?"

"Ostrich ferns! I'd better be able to fly," said the dragon, stiffly flapping his gold-colored wings. He hobbled along the beach, gave a little jump, and fluttered up to the top of the cliff. "I'm not the dragon I used to be," he panted, "but I'll get you home yet, Elmer. Don't you worry about that."

"Oh, I know you will. I'm not the least bit worried," said Elmer, although he had secretly hoped to find people on the island, and a boat going home, and all sorts of good things to eat.

Chapter Five

FLUTE, THE CANARY

Elmer and the dragon rested awhile on top of the cliff, watching the waves spreading out over the sand bar. Suddenly a little voice chirped, "You're Elmer Elevator, aren't you?"

Elmer was too startled to answer.

"Aren't you? Of course, it has been three years, and people do change."

Elmer looked all around but he couldn't see anybody. "Yes, I'm Elmer, but who and where are you?" he asked.

"Look up in the tree above you. It's me, Flute."

Elmer and the dragon looked up and there he was, Flute the canary—funny little Flute with two black

eyebrows and one black feather in each wing.

"Oh, Flute! How glad I am to see you. But how did you get here?"

"I flew here the day you let me out of my cage when your mother went to answer the doorbell. This is where all the escaped canaries live—Feather Island, we call it. But what on earth are you doing here?"

"Well, I just rescued this baby dragon, and he was flying me home, only we got caught in a storm and landed here instead. And now he's got to rest and get plenty of food and water before we can go on."

"Does he eat canaries?"

"I should say not!" snorted the dragon. "Only fruits and vegetables and lollipops."

"That's a relief," said Flute. "I almost didn't talk to you because the rest of the canaries were afraid. I'll just tell them everything's all right," and Flute trilled loudly in every direction. Soon canaries were chirping all over the island, and the pine trees rustled with fluttering wings.

"Let's go eat," said the dragon, who was bored and still hungry and thirsty. So Flute flew down and rode on Elmer's shoulder as they walked through the pines.

"Tell me, Flute, do people live on this island?" asked Elmer.

"No. Just canaries."

"That's what I thought. Well, how have you been getting along without my mother? She's never stopped worrying about you."

"Quite well, thank you," said Flute, "but I'm beginning to suffer from the island disease."

"What's that?"

"I know it sounds silly, but the whole island is sick with curiosity, and old King Can is actually dying of it."

"Who's King Can?" asked the dragon, becoming somewhat interested.

"He's the king of the canaries. He's really King

Can XI. His ancestors, King and Queen Can I, were the first canaries to live on the island. They came with a party of settlers. But the settlers sailed away after a month or two, and they left King Can and his wife behind."

"Now I understand about the ladder and the bucket and pine trees and the apple orchard," said Elmer.

"Yes," said Flute, "they are the work of the settlers. But to continue: Migrating birds often stop by here and King Can, being lonesome, told them to ask escaped canaries to live on his island. But even after many canaries had come, he was never well or happy. And when the other birds asked 'Why not?' King Can would answer, 'I'm dying of curiosity.' Pretty soon, the other canaries grew curious to know why he was so curious, but he told the reason only to his eldest son. And so they all grew sick with curiosity. Finally, when King Can I was a very old canary, he did die of curiosity and his eldest son became King Can II."

"Skunk cabbage! I smell skunk cabbage," interrupted the dragon right in the middle of the story, because by this time they had come out onto the meadow.

"It's right over there in the swamp," said Elmer, and the dragon lumbered off to eat and to drink cold water.

"King Can II, III, IV, V, VI, VII, VIII, IX, and X all died of curiosity as very old canaries, and now King Can XI is sick with it. And the rest of us are sick, too. I tell you, it's an awful thing," continued Flute.

"I suppose so," said Elmer. "I wonder what they could have been so curious about."

"See, there you go getting curious! What a great day it will be when this island gets over the plague of curiosity!"

"Maybe I could help King Can XI," suggested Elmer. "If *he* weren't curious anymore, then nobody else would be curious to know *why* he's curious, and everybody would get well."

"That's right," said Flute. "Let's go see the King. He lives in the biggest tree in the forest."

Elmer yelled to the dragon that he'd be back soon, but all he could hear was loud munching and drinking noises in the bushes.

Chapter Six

KING CAN XI

Flute perched on Elmer's shoulder and together they went to the biggest tree in the forest. Flute flew up into the branches and Elmer heard him chirp, "Good morning, Queen Can. An old friend of mine has just arrived on the island, and I'd like to introduce him to the King."

"Is that your friend down there?" asked the sleek tiny Queen suspiciously.

"Yes. He let me out of my cage back in Never-green City."

"The King isn't feeling well, you know."

"I know, that's why I want to introduce my friend. I think he can help the King, perhaps."

"Well, I'll go see if he's receiving visitors. You wait here."

Soon the Queen flew back all flustered. "The King will be down right away. I was really surprised. He's never before been so eager to see anyone!"

Elmer felt flattered, and quickly tucked in his shirt and straightened his cap.

Suddenly the King flew out of the branches and landed at Elmer's feet. Elmer was disappointed. The King looked just like a canary, only bigger and fluffier than the others.

"This is my dear friend Elmer Elevator," said Flute.

"Hello. Won't you sit down?" said King Can XI.
"Thank you," said Elmer, squatting down on the
pine needles.

"It's a great honor to have you on our island," said the King.

"It's a great honor to be here," said Elmer.

"The Queen said that Flute said that you might be able to help me. Is that right?" asked the King.

"Yes," said Elmer. "I thought perhaps I could help you to find out whatever you're so curious to know, and then all the other birds wouldn't be curious to know *why* you're curious, and everybody would get well."

"Hmm," said the King. "Did you have some special plan?"

"You'd have to help by telling me what's bothering you," said Elmer.

"That's what I was afraid of! Why, this has been a family secret ever since my great-great-great-great-great-great-great-great-grandfather was a young canary. No, I couldn't possibly tell you!" snorted King Can XI.

"Then I can't help you after all," said Elmer, getting up. "I'm sorry I bothered Your Majesty about it. Good-bye."

Elmer and Flute sadly started back through the pines.

"Ah, just a moment," called the King. "Maybe we could work out something. I'm awfully tired of being curious. Yes, by gosh, I believe I *will* tell you. But don't you dare tell anyone else!"

"I promise," said Elmer.

"Flute, go up and chatter with the Queen. Your friend and I wish to be alone."

The King whispered to Elmer, "You can't imagine how hard it is for me to tell you our family secret."

"I'm sure it's extremely difficult," said Elmer helpfully.

"Well, the secret is—the secret is—the secret is—oh, I can't tell you now. Could you come back at sundown? I just can't say it in the bright sunlight."

"I understand," said Elmer, "and I'll be glad to come back later." He called to Flute, who had been trying hard not to yawn in front of the Queen, and together they went to find the dragon.

"Well, did you see the King?" asked the dragon, who was resting comfortably beside the pool, his stomach bulging with skunk cabbages and ostrich ferns.

"Yes, but now I'm really curious. I'm to go back at sundown and then he's going to tell me the secret. It's a very old family secret."

"I just can't stand it! I can't stand it!" said Flute. "Oh, I'll be so glad to be rid of the curiosity plague."

"I'll do my best," said Elmer, taking a long drink of water and settling down beside the dragon to eat eight tangerines.

Elmer and the dragon fell fast asleep while Flute went all over the island spreading the news and waiting for sundown.

Chapter Seven

THE SECRET

"Wake up! Wake up! It's time to see the King!" chirped Flute as the red sun settled over the meadow. Elmer opened his eyes and forgot for a moment where he was. Then he jumped up and put on his knapsack.

"I want to come, too," yawned the dragon.

"You weren't invited," said Flute.

"Neither were you, Flute, come to think of it," said Elmer.

"Let's all go and see what happens," suggested the

dragon. So off they went to see the King. He was waiting for them at the foot of the very tall tree, nervously hopping from one foot to the other, pecking at imaginary mosquitoes.

"What's that?" he asked, pointing to the dragon.

"That's my good friend the baby dragon. I rescued him two days ago and now he's taking me home."

"I don't like him," said the King, feeling small and helpless.

"Oh, yes you do!" said Flute.

"Quiet, Flute! I guess I know what I like and what I don't!"

The dragon drooped his head and began to back away.

"Oh, well," said the King, "come on back. If I'm going to tell the secret to anyone, it'll never be a secret anymore, and I suppose you might as well know, too. I do wish it weren't such an old secret."

Flute, the dragon, and Elmer waited quietly while

the King looked at the ground, then up at the tree, and then down at the ground.

"Treasure!" he whispered so suddenly that they all jumped into the air. "At least I think it's treasure, but I can't find out without your help."

"Where?" asked Elmer.

"It's—it's—it's not very far from here," said the King. Elmer, Flute, and the dragon looked every-which-way to see where the treasure could be.

"Oh gosh, I guess I'll have to tell you where, too," said poor old King Can XI. "It's buried—it's buried right under this tree—in a big iron chest."

"What sort of treasure?" asked Elmer.

"That's what I'm dying of curiosity to know," said the King.

"So that's it!" sighed Flute.

"And you're sure this is the right tree?" asked Elmer.

"Absolutely! You see, it's much bigger than the

others, and that's because it was the only one here when the settlers came. They planted the other pines and the apple orchard so they'd have wood and food when they returned. But they never came back, and their chest is still buried right here."

Everybody waited for the King to continue, but he didn't, so Elmer said, "Let's dig it up!"

"Yes, let's!" echoed Flute.

"All right," said the King. "My secret's all spoiled now, anyway. You'll find the shovel under that rock."

"What shovel?" asked Elmer.

"The settlers left a shovel over there. It's rusty by now, but it's probably better than nothing."

Elmer went to get the shovel while the King danced around on the pine needles chirping, "I'm feeling better already." The Queen kept tittering and muttering to herself, "I never thought I'd live to see this day."

"Now, where should I begin digging?" asked Elmer.

"It's a rhyme," said the King. "It goes like this:
Four shovel lengths from the trunk of the pine,
Making the rock the guide for the line."

Elmer carefully measured the distance and began to dig. The dragon did his best to help while Flute and the King and Queen sat watching the hole growing deeper. By now it was dark in the pine forest, but enough moonlight filtered through the branches of the tall trees so that they could just see what they were doing. They dug for six hours without ever hitting a root or a rock or anything like an iron chest.

"Are you certain this is the right place?" asked Elmer, tired and discouraged.

"I'm positive!" said the King. Just then the moon went under the clouds and Elmer's shovel hit something with a loud clang.

"The chest!" they all shouted, but it was too dark to see. And they waited so long for the moon to come out that they all went to sleep still waiting.

Chapter Eight

TREASURE

Flute woke up and trilled so loudly that he startled
the King and the Queen and Elmer and the dragon
wide awake. The other canaries had been up for an
hour and were crowding around to see what was happening under the tree. Everybody peered into the big
hole and gasped, "A real treasure chest, with a ring

134

in the top! But how will we ever get it out?"

The King looked at Elmer, and Elmer looked at the dragon. "Dragon, do you think you could put your tail through the ring and pull up the chest?"

"I'll try," said the dragon, puffing up with importance as the swarms of canaries moved aside for him. He backed up to the hole, stuck his tail down and through the ring, and pulled.

Nothing happened.

"Couldn't you pull harder?" suggested the King.

"That's exactly what I was going to try. Just let me catch my breath," said the dragon somewhat crossly. "After all, I'm not used to lifting heavy chests with my tail." He took a deep, deep breath and pulled very, very hard, and suddenly the chest moved. He grunted and strained and struggled and panted and slowly, slowly hoisted the chest up out of the hole.

"Far enough!" yelled Elmer. "Now walk forward

and set it down."

Crash! The chest fell down on the pine needles and the dragon staggered off to sit down while the canaries shouted "Bravo!"

"Quiet! Quiet!" yelled King Can XI. "I am now about to tell you the last part of the secret. The key to this chest—the key to this chest—well, anyway, this is the last part of the secret. My illustrious ancestor, King Can I, stole the key from the settlers, and the key to this chest is in my nest. Go get it, Flute. No, never mind. I'll go get it myself."

The King flew up to his nest and down again with a big brass key in his beak. Elmer pried out the dirt in the keyhole with his jackknife and put in the key.

Click! The lock turned. Elmer threw back the lid, and picked up a note lying on top of a piece of heavy canvas. "Can you read what it says?" asked the King.

"Yes," said Elmer, feeling sick with excitement as he read the note aloud:

This chest was left here by Oliver Hinckle, for the purpose of helping him and his friends to settle on this island when he returns. In the event that he does not return to find the chest himself, the chest becomes the property of whosoever discovers it.

The following is a list of the items herein buried:

12 pewter plates
 6 pewter cups
12 table settings - sterling silver
 1 iron skillet
 2 iron pots, with lids
 1 coffee mill

"Rubbish!" interrupted the King. "Isn't there anything but cooking utensils?"

"Let me finish the list," said Elmer. He continued reading:

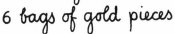 can each of salt and sugar

1 axe

1 tinder box

5 bags seed, including squash, corn, cabbage, wheat and millet

1 gold watch and chain, belonging to my wife Sarah

1 sterling silver harmonica

6 bags of gold pieces

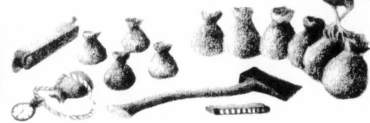

"Gold! I knew it! Just think of it, Queen. Six bags of gold!" trilled the King.

"What will you do with them, King dear?" asked the Queen.

"I won't do anything with them. I'll just have them and be rich."

"Shall I unpack now?" asked Elmer, who was anxious to see the sterling silver harmonica.

"By all means," ordered King Can XI, strutting back and forth in front of the twittering canaries.

Elmer unpacked everything, and at last came to the sterling silver harmonica. He blew on it gently, and the sound was so sweet that all the canaries stopped chattering and listened. The King listened, too, with tears in his eyes. When Elmer had finished playing "The Bear Went Over the Mountain," the King flew up to a branch of the pine and said solemnly, "Elmer, on behalf of the Queen and myself, and all the other Feather Islanders, I want to thank you and your

dragon friend for digging up this treasure and thereby ridding us of the plague of curiosity. I now present you with that silver harmonica, which you play so beautifully, and three of the six bags of gold. And to this brave dragon I present the gold watch and chain. Elmer, fasten it around his neck."

Elmer hooked the chain around the dragon's neck, arranging the watch at his throat. "How's that?" asked Elmer.

"I can't see it, but it feels just fine," said the proud baby dragon.

The birds all clapped their wings and then the

dragon, who really didn't care for speeches, re-marked, "Looking at those pots and plates makes me hungry. Let's celebrate and eat something!"

"Goodness!" said the Queen. "I don't believe we've ever had a celebration before. What shall we eat?"

"Tangerines!" said Elmer. "I bet you've never tasted one."

Elmer peeled twelve of the thirty-one tangerines he had left in his knapsack, and put one on each of the twelve pewter plates. Then he hurried off to pick a good mess of skunk cabbages and ostrich ferns for the dragon. When he came back everyone crowded around to feast. Elmer sat beside the dragon and ate nine tangerines all by himself. Then he played "Turkey in the Straw" on the sterling silver harmon-ica while the King did a jig on a pewter plate. Soon everybody joined in the dancing, and they danced themselves to sleep, all over the pine needles under the great tall tree.

Chapter Nine

FAREWELL

"I think I ought to be getting home," said Elmer the next morning as he ate the last ten tangerines. "How do you feel, Dragon?"

"Fine! Why, I could fly to the moon and back."

"Good," said Elmer, "because I think today is my father's birthday." He looked at the plates and the pots and the cups and the silverware and the bags of seed spread all over the pine needles and asked, "King, what shall we do with your part of the treasure?"

"Dear, dear," said the King. "Well, we can plant the seeds, but I guess we ought to put the rest back in the chest. But my gold! I must have my gold!"

"I insist upon at least one silver spoon," cheeped the Queen.

"Then I'll save out the seeds and a spoon and three pieces of gold," suggested Elmer, who was anxious to be off.

"Better make it five pieces of gold," said the King. "I really ought to give one to Flute."

Elmer packed the chest and gave the key back to the King. "Shall we bury it again?" he asked.

"I suppose so," said the King with tears in his eyes. "I hate to think of it way down there, but at least it will be safe from robbers. But never mind about putting back the dirt. We can do that ourselves."

So the dragon carefully lowered the chest into the
hole while Elmer put away the shovel. Then Elmer
packed his knapsack with the three bags of gold and
the sterling silver harmonica, carefully wrapping the
harmonica in the burlap bag left over from the rescue.

"Good-bye, everybody, and thanks for a wonderful visit," he shouted to all the canaries. "You can
count on me. I'll never tell your secret to a soul."

"Good-bye, Elmer, and thanks again," said the
King, who was already busy giving orders to the
other canaries about filling up the hole.

Flute rode on Elmer's shoulder as he and the
dragon walked back to the cliff. "Good-bye, Elmer.
Please give my best to your mother. She really was
awfully good to me, you know."

"I will, Flute, and good-bye," said Elmer, wondering if he didn't have some little thing to give Flute.
He looked once more in his knapsack and found that
he still had three sticks of chewing gum and half a

package of rubber bands. "I don't suppose you'd like to have these?" he asked.

"I'd love them," said Flute. "I'll keep them with my gold piece, and I'll be even richer than the King because I'll keep my treasure where I can see it every day."

Flute told Elmer and the dragon the best way to fly to Nevergreen City, and then Elmer hopped aboard, waving farewell to Flute and Feather Island.

Chapter Ten

ELMER FLIES HOME

They flew and flew, the dragon trying hard not to look at, or think about, the wet, wet ocean. Elmer sat watching their shadow rippling over the waves beneath them, feeling washed by the cool morning breeze. The dragon was strong and well rested, being nicely stuffed with skunk cabbages and ostrich ferns, and they hadn't stopped once when he shouted towards evening, "I think I see land ahead!"

"So do I, and I think it's the coast of Popsicornia," yelled Elmer. "Yes, I'm sure it is. There's Firefly Lighthouse. It won't be long now. It's just a few miles up the coast from here."

"Where shall I land when we get there?" asked the

153

dragon. "Now that I'm free I should hate to be put in a zoo or a circus or something."

"Well, it'll be dark soon. I think you could land on a wharf without attracting attention. Of course, we'll have to be quiet."

They flew up the coast, passing the lighthouse and the Village of Fruitoria and the Town of Custard, and finally came to the outskirts of Nevergreen City.

"There it is!" cried Elmer. "See, that dark patch is Evergreen Park. I live just across the street. Could you land on that long wharf just ahead?"

"I think so," said the dragon, "but I do hope nobody sees me." He circled lower and lower and landed gently on the end of the wharf. Elmer slid off and whispered, "Gosh, it was fun knowing you. I'm going to miss you and flying and everything, and thanks so much for bringing me home."

"It was fun, wasn't it," sniffled the dragon, "and I'll never forget how you came all the way to Wild Island just to rescue me. By the way, Elmer, I really think you ought to have this beautiful gold watch and chain. I can't see it on me, and anyway, I don't even know how to tell time."

"Are you sure? I could give it to my mother. But haven't I got something you'd like to trade it for?"

"Well, as a matter of fact, I was wondering if you still had some of those delicious pink lollipops."

"I have four left over," said Elmer, getting them out and taking off the wrappers. "Would you like all four at once?"

"Yes," said the dragon.

They stood there quietly in the dark, the dragon sucking four pink lollipops, and Elmer whispered, "Where will you go from here?"

"I'll go to find my family in the great high mountains of Blueland," said the dragon, thinking of his six sisters and seven brothers and his gigantic mother and father.

"I'd like to go there too, someday," said Elmer.

"Well, maybe you will, but listen—I hear voices."

"Men coming down the wharf! Quick, you'd better hurry! Good-bye, dear Dragon."

The dragon flew up into the darkness just as two watchmen thumped by to make their rounds. Elmer hid behind a crate and heard one say, "Funny, I was sure I heard voices, and I know I heard something big flying just over our heads."

"Look! Four lollipop wrappers!" said the other watchman, who had been searching the wharf with a lantern.

"Hmm," said the first watchman, and then they walked back down the wharf. Elmer followed them at a distance, and while they were telling another watchman about the lollipop wrappers he ran as fast as he could, through the streets, through Evergreen Park,

all the way home. He leaped up the porch steps three at a time yelling, "Mother, Daddy, I'm home! Happy Birthday!"

Mr. and Mrs. Elevator rushed to the door and threw their arms around Elmer. "Oh, Elmer, how glad we are to see you! You don't know how worried we've been these past two weeks. Where on earth did you go?"

"I had an important job to do," said Elmer, staring at the living-room sofa. "Why, there's my friend the old alley cat!"

"Yes," said Mrs. Elevator. "As much as I've always hated cats, I just didn't have the heart to turn her out. She came to the door the day after you left, and I kept thinking, 'Elmer loved this cat. I really ought to take good care of her.' And do you know, I've grown awfully fond of her in just two weeks."

Elmer rushed over to the cat and whispered, "I rescued the dragon and he just flew me home. He was right where you told me he'd be."

"You did what?" asked Mr. Elevator.

"Oh, nothing," said Elmer. "By the way, here's your birthday present." Elmer gave his father the three bags of gold and played "Happy Birthday" on the sterling silver harmonica. "And here's a beautiful gold watch and chain for you, Mother."

"But where did you ever get these things?" gasped Mr. and Mrs. Elevator.

"That's a secret I can never tell," said Elmer, rummaging in the icebox for something to eat.

THE END

The
DRAGONS OF BLUELAND

Chapter One

THE HIDING PLACE

Over the harbor, past the lighthouse, away from Nevergreen City flew the happy baby dragon. "I'm on my way home to the great high mountains of Blueland!" he shouted to the evening skies. "At last I'm off to find my six sisters and seven brothers, and my dear gigantic mother and father."

He sped northward over the coast of Popsicornia. He flew all night through the dark scudding clouds toward Awful Desert, which surrounded the mountains of Blueland. "I must be careful," he thought to himself, "that nobody sees me on my way, but I'll have to stop and rest somewhere. Where can I hide? I've grown as big as a buffalo, and my blue-and-yellow

stripes and gold-colored wings will certainly attract attention."

The darkness faded into morning, and looking down he saw green meadows, fields of corn and potatoes, a road wandering past barns and houses, and a brook zigzagging back and forth across the road. "Perhaps I can find a bridge to hide under," thought the dragon, "but I'll have to hurry. Soon the farmers will be up."

He swooped, and coasted down to a place where the road crossed the brook. Gently he landed and pattered down the bank to hide underneath the bridge. But there wasn't any bridge! The road had been built right over the brook, and the water flowed under the road through a culvert, a long round tunnel. And the culvert was too small for a dragon to hide in.

"I'll try another crossing," he said to himself, scrambling up the bank, and galloping down the road as fast as he could to the next crossing. But here, too, a very small culvert carried the water under the road.

"Oh dear, oh dear!" he muttered as he galloped on farther between a yellow farmhouse and a big yellow barn. Just as he was passing he heard a rooster scream and a window slam shut in the house. "Where shall I hide? Where shall I hide?" he panted.

And then he came to a third crossing. He tumbled down the bank and found another culvert, but a big culvert, big enough for a baby dragon to hide in. He crawled inside, wading through shallow water that cooled his hot, sandy feet.

"What if someone in the farmhouse saw me?" he kept thinking as he stretched just far enough to nibble the tasty skunk cabbages and marsh marigolds growing outside the culvert. And then as he ate and cooled off, he felt tired and happy and almost safe, and he dozed off to sleep in the culvert.

Chapter Two

MR. AND MRS. WAGONWHEEL

But someone *had* seen the dragon. At least he was sure he'd seen something blue and yellow and gold galloping down the road. It was Mr. Wagonwheel, the farmer living in the yellow farmhouse, who had just been closing his window as the dragon ran past.

"What's that galloping noise?" asked Mrs. Wagonwheel, sitting up in bed.

"A large blue monster just ran by, and after breakfast I'm going to find out all about it!" yelled Mr.

Wagonwheel, jumping into his clothes and rushing off to put the cows in the barn for milking.

Mrs. Wagonwheel, meanwhile, made pancakes and coffee, but forgot to boil the eggs. She was horribly upset at the thought of a monster rushing past her house at five o'clock in the morning.

Mr. Wagonwheel hurried through the milking, let the cows into the pasture, and dashed back to the kitchen. He was anxious to eat and be off after the Blue Demon, as he had decided to call whatever it was. He swallowed a pancake whole and banged two eggs on the side of his cup.

Splop! Raw egg flew all over the table and Mr. Wagonwheel. Mrs. Wagonwheel had forgotten to boil the eggs, of course.

"Martha! What's the matter with you?" yelled Mr. Wagonwheel.

"Oh, I'm sorry," said poor Mrs. Wagonwheel. "I'm so upset about that horrible monster I don't know what

I'm doing," and she nervously slipped a pancake instead of her handkerchief into her apron pocket.

"Well, boil more eggs!" roared Mr. Wagonwheel, going to the sink to wash off his face and hands and shirt and overalls.

Now Mr. Wagonwheel liked his eggs hard, very

hard, and as he waited for them to get very hard, it began to rain. It was only a drizzly rain, but enough to wash away the dragon's footprints in the dusty road.

"Drat it!" thundered Mr. Wagonwheel, looking out the window. "It's raining!"

"I thought we needed rain, dear," said Mrs. Wagonwheel.

"We do, but why can't it wait until I capture the Blue Demon? Now maybe I'll never find him."

"Maybe it's just as well," said Mrs. Wagonwheel, carefully putting a spoonful of salt in her coffee.

"Well, I can see you have no spirit of adventure," grumped Mr. Wagonwheel, peeling his at-last-ready very hard eggs.

He picked up his rifle, a strong rope, and put on his raincoat and boots. "I'm off!" he yelled, and slammed the door.

"He'll never come back," thought Mrs. Wagonwheel, and she quietly sat down to cry.

Mr. Wagonwheel ran down the road, pouncing on bushes, peering behind trees, and examining roadside ditches, yelling all the while, "Coming, ready or not!" He made such a racket that the cows heard him in plenty of time. They huddled around the big culvert where the baby dragon was hiding and pretended to be busy drinking water. For they had found the sleeping dragon while Mr. Wagonwheel was eating his very hard eggs.

"Wake up!" they had said, "and tell us what you are, and what you're doing in our culvert."

The dragon woke up with a start, and then smiled at the friendly cows. "I'm a baby dragon," he explained, "and I'm on my way home to the great high mountains of Blueland."

"But what are you doing in our culvert?" asked a cow.

"I'm hiding. You see, most people think that there are

no dragons left, and if I should be captured, I'd surely end up in a zoo or a circus, and never get home again."

"Sh!" said another cow. "I think I hear Mr. Wagonwheel now. All through milking time he was muttering about catching a Blue Demon. He must have meant you."

It was then that the cows huddled around the opening to the culvert, and the dragon crouched down on his stomach in the water.

"The culvert!" yelled Mr. Wagonwheel, brandishing his rifle. "An excellent hiding place for the Blue Demon." And he started down the bank on the other side of the road.

"It's all over now," thought the dragon, who could tell where the farmer was from the noise he was making. But just then Mr. Wagonwheel looked across the road at his peaceful cows and thought, "My cows would be in a panic if the Demon were hiding here!" He turned back up the bank and ran down the road, beating the bushes and peering behind trees.

The cows grazed nearby all day long, talking to the dragon and telling him when it was safe to come out of the culvert. Toward evening they heard Mr. Wagonwheel stamping back along the road, yelling "Hoop-la! All of you, into the barn!" and as they wandered off they quietly warned the dragon, "Leave just as soon as he goes to the barn. It's just like him to be out looking for you by flashlight after supper."

And they were right. Long after the dragon had flown far beyond the yellow farmhouse and culvert, Mr. Wagonwheel was shooting into bushes. Mrs. Wagonwheel was in bed with a case of nerves.

Chapter Three

THE MEN ON THE SLOPE

"It's a lovely night for flying," thought the dragon as he hurried toward the north, urged on by cool brisk winds. The rain had stopped long ago, and a crescent moon shone palely. Looking down, he could see the outline of Seaweed Bay, and then a point of land called Due East Lookout. At this point he must turn and fly directly westward over Seaweed City, across Spiky Mountain Range, and over Awful Desert to reach the Blueland Mountains in the heart of the desert. Many people had tried to cross the desert and climb these mountains, but there was no water, and treacherous sandstorms raged all year round, making traveling almost impossible. So far, no man had succeeded.

"It won't be long now!" sang the baby dragon as he passed over Seaweed City, over the coastal Spiky Mountain Range, and then started over Awful Desert beyond.

"What a lovely night!" he thought again. And then, all of a sudden, he realized how clear it was over the desert. "Where are the sandstorms? Yes, where are the sandstorms?" A sick feeling came over him. In weather like this a man might be able to cross the desert into Blueland, might see one of the dragon

family, and learn the dragon secret, *that dragons still
live in Blueland!*

Faster and faster he flew, and way up ahead he saw
a tiny light where the mountains rose straight up out
of the desert.

"Men!" thought the dragon. "If only I'm in time to
warn my family."

Onward he sped until he could see that the light was
the blaze of a campfire on the rocky mountain slope.

He counted four or five men sitting around the campfire.

"I'd better find out what they're planning to do so I'll know how to save my family," thought the dragon, circling down and landing below the men. He carefully picked his way through the huge rocks on the slope and hid close enough to hear what the men were saying.

"If Frank and Albert and the rest don't find water soon, we're sunk. We'll have to get back pretty quick, and what if the weather changes? After all, this is the first time, so far as anybody knows, that the weather has ever been clear over the desert, and I don't trust it to last very long."

"Me neither," said another voice.

Just then they heard a shout farther up the slope and a man came running down toward the fire.

"Did you find water?" they asked him.

"Water! Loads of it. The mountains form a circle,

and all the streams from these mountains flow toward the center to make a tremendous lake. But that's not all we found!"

"You mean you found evidence that the great dragons of Blueland actually did exist at one time?"

"Evidence!" said the man who had run down the slope. "Evidence! Why, we've got fifteen of the most beautiful dragons you ever dreamed of trapped in a cave that seems to have only one entrance. The rest of the men are guarding it."

"Fifteen trapped in the cave!" moaned the baby dragon. "Why, that's my whole family—my six sisters, seven brothers and my dear gigantic mother and father. I'm the only one left to save them. But why didn't they fly away?" He listened to the men again.

"How do you know you have fifteen in a cave?"

"We took them by surprise. They were asleep at the entrance, and when they saw us they rushed inside. What a sight!"

"Fifteen dragons!" One of the men whistled. "What did they look like?"

"They went so fast it was hard to see, but there was one huge blue one, a big yellow one, about five smaller green ones, and the rest were blue and yellow. They all had red horns and feet, and gold-colored wings!"

"I can't wait," said one of the men. "Why, every zoo in the country will want one!"

"Oh, no!" groaned the horrified baby dragon, hiding behind the rocks.

Chapter Four

IN THE CAVE

As the men went about packing up knapsacks and putting out the fire, the dragon carefully crept up the mountain slope. "It's a good thing they don't know that the cave does have another entrance, but I wonder if I can still squeeze through it."

It was the tunnel through which he had gone when he ran away to sit on the cloud. At that time, only he and his two youngest sisters were small enough to fit into it. "Maybe, just maybe, I can still get through," he thought.

He hurried up the dry rocky slope of the mountain, racing to get to the tunnel before the sun broke over the rim of the desert. "I've got to rescue them!" he

thought frantically. Over the gap between two snow-capped peaks he galloped and then down into the beautiful green alpine meadows in the center of the mountain circle. Here, streams babbled down the slopes to a bottomless lake. Masses of wild flowers, gentians, butterfly weed, painted cup, all colors,

paraded along the brooksides. In the pastures, every-where, were giant snapdragon plants looking more like bushes than flowers, but the dragon did not have time to stop and gaze at his beautiful home in the great high mountains of Blueland. Already the sun was reaching over the horizon, lighting up the sky.

"Here it is," he panted and he dove into a thick clump of snapdragons growing over the entrance to the small tunnel. He had seen the men across the lake guarding the cave with an enormous net. "I wish I knew what they're planning to do next," he thought. "But it's too late now. I'll have to wait until dark."

He tried to pass into the tunnel, but the roots of the snapdragons had grown over the entrance, and dirt had washed in from above. "Dig carefully. They might notice the stir in the bushes," he warned himself as he cleared the way. At last he could fit into the hole, and he started the long trip through the tunnel.

"I might get stuck any moment," he groaned as the tunnel turned corners and gradually dug deeper into the side of the mountain, always only just big enough for him to squeeze through.

On and on he crawled, and just when he thought he would surely get to the large part of the cave, he got stuck. He pushed and wiggled, but he could not get through. Tears rolled down his blue cheeks. "I wanted so badly to see my family," he sniffled. "But maybe they're near enough to hear me now," and he whispered, "Mother, Father, are you there?"

"Who's that?" asked a voice that sounded like his sister Eustacia's.

"It's Boris!" cried his mother. "Oh, Boris, Boris! We thought we'd never see you again. Come on into the cave. We're in terrible danger."

"I know," said Boris the dragon. "But I can't squeeze through the tunnel. Oh, I do wish I could.

But listen, whatever you do, don't go near the main entrance to the cave. Many men are waiting there with an enormous net. I don't know yet what they plan to do with it, but I'll try to find out tonight if nothing happens before then. I think they're afraid to come in and get you. They don't know how harmless we really are. Anyway, keep calm and count on me. I have a

friend who may be able to help, and if you don't hear from me soon, it'll be because I've gone off to get him. Now I'll have to back out again. I must stay near the tunnel entrance so I can get out easily when I have a chance. Goodbye!"

And Boris backed out for what seemed like hours and hours until he came out among the roots of the snapdragon bushes. He peered through the leaves across the lake and counted sixteen men standing in a row outside the cave. A breeze sprang up across the lake and carried their voices over the water to him.

"They'll come out when they get hungry enough," said one man.

"But how do you know they won't be fiercer when they're hungry and have been trapped for some time? Me, I'd rather go in after them right now."

"Go in after them?" said a third man. "Why, we don't even know anything about that cave. Suppose it does have more entrances? The dragons may have escaped already. And what about pitfalls and rockslides in there? We ought to know more about this. No, the thing to do is to leave ten men here on guard, and send the other six to search for other entrances and to have a look at the rock formation around here."

"Good idea!" said the man who had come down the mountain to the campfire.

The wind changed and the dragon could only hear confused sounds of talking, but the men seemed to be deciding who would stay and who would go.

"They'll find me for sure if I stay here, and I don't want to trap myself too," thought the dragon. "Daylight or no, I'd better fly and get Elmer. He'll know what to do, if we can get back in time."

Quickly he fitted the snapdragon roots over the tunnel hole, arranging them carefully so they wouldn't look newly dug-up. Then, keeping close to the ground, he crept through the green meadows and up, up, up to the gap between the mountain peaks. He took one last look at the beautiful blue lake surrounded by the green, green meadows, felt quite sure he hadn't been seen, and then plunged down the rocky slope on the other side. Up in the air he flew, shielded from the eyes of the men by the circle of mountains.

Chapter Five

BACK TO NEVERGREEN CITY

High, high over the desert flew the dragon, the hot wind stifling him, the hot sun parching his throat. He strained his eyes to see each object on the sands to make sure it wasn't a man.

At last he was over Spiky Mountain Range. Panting for air and water, he circled down fast and plunged through the trees to a mountain brook. He had seen no one on the desert.

"I'll rest here until dusk," he thought, sticking his head right under the cool, gurgling water. Then he lay down in the brook on his stomach, carefully keeping his gold-colored wings out of the water. As he dried off on a sunny rock he listened for noises of men and dreamed of how he and Elmer would rescue his family. Once he heard children's voices, but a woman called them together and they went off in the other direction.

"School picnic," he thought as he shook out his wings for the long, hard trip ahead. He wanted to reach Nevergreen City by morning without stopping.

Up through the trees and over Seaweed City flew the dragon. He saw lights popping on suddenly along streets, in houses, but he didn't hear a little boy scream, "Mommy, come look at the dragon in the sky!"

It didn't matter. The little boy's mother only said, "Chester, I told you to stay in bed!" So Chester was the only one to see the dragon, and nobody believed him until later when the "dragon affair" had become famous.

"As I remember, Elmer said he lived right across the street from a park," thought the dragon as he hurried on. "Yes, it was Evergreen Park, but what if I can't find him?"

The wind beat back his tears as he raced over Seaweed Bay, over Mr. Wagonwheel's farm and the zigzagging brook. He thought he could see the road as the moon slipped in and out among the clouds.

He flew to the coast of Popsicornia and followed it southward. Suddenly he felt flooded in light. What had happened? The moon? No. He looked down and saw a beam of light leaping up from a ship off the coast. He violently zigzagged up and down, to one side and then to the other, trying to get rid of the light.

Men were shouting on the ship. Into the beam, out again, flooded in light, out of the beam again he flew. He knew that the ship's searchlight had found him accidentally, but as it tried to follow his flight he thought wildly, "How well can they see me? What do they think I am?"

And then, as suddenly as the light had found him, it lost him. He sped on in the comforting darkness, his heart pounding hard with fright.

As dawn began to break into the sky he saw Never-green City harbor, the lighthouse, and in the center of the city, a large green shape.

"Evergreen Park," he thought with relief, and he quietly glided down among the trees. No one had been on the streets to see him.

Chapter Six

ELMER TO THE RESCUE

Dawn brought Saturday to Nevergreen City and as Elmer slept snugly in his comfortable bed he was suddenly awakened by a damp cold kiss on his cheek.

"Wake up, wake up!" insisted a voice.

He opened his eyes and muttered, "It's Saturday. No school today."

"Elmer, wake up!" said the old alley cat, the same old alley cat that had told him all about the dragon and how to rescue him. "Elmer, we've got work to do. I just saw the dragon fly into the park. He must be in trouble. We'll have to hurry to find him a hiding place before the city wakes up."

"The dragon! Why, he only just brought me home!" Elmer jumped out of bed and into his clothes, and tip-toed down the stairs with the cat following behind.

Silently they crept out the front door, down the porch steps and into Evergreen Park. "You look this way. I'll go down the other way," said the cat.

"Where could a dragon hide?" wondered Elmer,
looking at the rows of trees along the walks, the scattered rocks, the pool, and then at the place where

the city was going to build an amusement center.
A big steam shovel sat idly on the spot marked out
for foundations. Elmer liked steam shovels and was
just thinking of exploring this one when the shovel
jiggled a bit.

"The dragon!" He climbed up quickly into the cab.

"Elmer!" whispered the baby dragon. "Oh, Elmer!" And the dragon burst into tears because he was so glad to see his friend.

"The alley cat saw you fly into the park," explained Elmer, hugging the dragon around the neck. "But why have you come back? Are you in trouble?"

"Terrible trouble," groaned the dragon, and he explained what had happened to his family. "You'll help me, won't you?" he pleaded.

"Of course," said Elmer. "Let's think out a plan. I suppose we'll have to wait until dark to leave."

"I suppose so," said the dragon sadly.

"But you'll be able to rest right here," said the cat, who had found them by this time. "It's Saturday, and the men won't start today. I'll keep meddlers away. Meanwhile, let's work on the plan."

The three friends discussed the problem all morning. Then Elmer went home for lunch. His mother was used to his long early morning walks, but she'd be suspicious if he didn't turn up for lunch.

That afternoon Elmer took all the money out of his tin bank and went to collect the things he would need. He bought:

16 whistles, of assorted tones

16 horns, of assorted tones

 1 cap pistol, with caps

 1 ball heavy string

 6 large chocolate bars

 3 boxes Fig Newtons

He found his very sharp jackknife, and took a flashlight from the kitchen drawer. Then he carefully packed everything in his father's knapsack and went down to supper. He had $7.36 left over from the shopping.

"Elmer, what have you been doing all day?" asked his mother. "I haven't seen hide nor hair of you except for lunch."

"Oh, I've been over in the park looking at the place where they're going to build the amusement center," said Elmer, which was true in a way.

At last the moment came to sneak out with his knapsack and join the dragon at the steam shovel. As he ran down the path he saw the old alley cat waiting for him. "I'm sorry you can't come, too," said Elmer, climbing onto the dragon's back.

"So am I," said the cat sadly. "But I'm too old. I'm better off taking care of your mother and father. They do worry so. Well, goodbye! Good luck!"

"Goodbye!" whispered Elmer and the dragon as they flew up into the air.

Chapter Seven

THE DRAGONS OF BLUELAND

"Tell me more about your family," said Elmer as the dragon flew over the harbor and northward along the coast of Popsicornia. "Do you all look alike?"

"Oh, no. We've all got gold-colored wings and red feet and horns, but my father is blue and my mother is yellow. All my six sisters are green, ranging from

yellow-green to blue-green. We boys are all both blue and yellow. I have wide stripes, but two brothers have narrow stripes, one with the stripes going the other way; one has yellow polka dots on blue, and one blue polka dots on yellow; one has a yellow head and body and one leg, with three blue legs and tail; one is speckled blue and yellow like a bird's egg; and the last has patches of blue and yellow."

"How wonderful! You must look like an Easter parade when you're all out together."

"I guess we do," said the dragon, "especially when

Father has us doing our exercises. He's a great one for exercises."

"Exercises?" said Elmer.

"You know, standing on your head and somersaults and leapfrog and all that sort of thing. Of course, in the summer we spend most of our time mowing the meadows and tending to the flowers. Each one of us has a special part of Blueland to take care of. I wonder what's become of my piece. I suppose Mother has taken it over. I had the marshy part near the lakeside. That's why I'm so particularly fond of marsh mari-

golds and skunk cabbages."

"But what about in the wintertime?" asked Elmer, looking down at the line of waves breaking against the rocky shore in the moonlight. "It must be very cold and snowy, and not much fun for exercising."

"Oh, we do our exercises summer and winter. Father sees to that, and of course we have lots of fun sliding down the mountain slopes onto the frozen lake. But the winter is really fun because we sit in a circle in our cave and Father tells us scary stories about knights. It seems there used to be lots of knights who rode about just looking for dragons. They captured and

killed most all of us, but a few escaped to Blueland. My father says his grandfather could remember the knights very well, with their heavy coats of armor and lances and swords and helmets."

"Oh, sure. I've read about them in books," said Elmer. "But those dragons were always fierce and about to eat up somebody."

"Nonsense," said the dragon. "That's just what the knights liked to make people believe, so everybody would think they were very brave when they went dragon hunting. Dragons look fierce sometimes, but they're really very gentle. That's why they finally ran

away to Blueland. They wanted to be left alone. And now more men have decided to bother us. Goodness knows what they'll do to us this time. If only we get back in time! We can't possibly make it before tomorrow evening. That will make it over two days since I left."

"Oh, we'll save your family all right," said Elmer hopefully. "I can't wait to see them all." He snuggled up against the baby dragon's neck and dreamed of the rescue as they sped through the night toward the mountains of Blueland.

Chapter Eight

TO SPIKY MOUNTAIN RANGE

"Where are we going to rest tomorrow?" asked Elmer, biting off a corner of a chocolate bar to help him stay awake.

"I'm trying to get all the way to Spiky Mountain Range," said the dragon. "No more Mr. Wagonwheel for me if I can help it. He's an awful..."

"A searchlight!" interrupted Elmer as a beam of light shot up from below, lighting up the dragon's gold-colored wings.

"It's from that ship, Elmer. They saw me last night, too. Hold on tight. I'm going to try to dodge it!" yelled the dragon, swooping, diving up and down, swerving from side to side.

Elmer grabbed the dragon's neck and held on as hard as he could. He didn't dare open his eyes, but he could hear men shouting on the ship.

"Right, move it to the right! Faster, faster!"

"Left, now! Hey! I think something's riding whatever it is!"

"Looks like a boy!" shouted another man.

And then the moon slipped behind a cloudbank. The dragon escaped the beam of light, and flew frantically through the darkness while the light danced over the sky still looking for them.

"Good work!" said Elmer, feeling very dizzy and quite sick.

"But they saw us, both of us," moaned the dragon.

"That's all right. They don't know where we're going, and we'll have your whole family rescued by the time they decide what we are," said Elmer, wondering if it would be wiser to finish eating his chocolate bar then or later. He was still feeling sickish.

"I hope you're right," muttered the dragon doubtfully.

On and on they flew until at dawn they were over Seaweed Bay and Due East Lookout. The dragon swung westward over Seaweed City and landed in a forest on Spiky Mountain Range. He was so tired that he fell asleep before he had time for a drink of water. Elmer finished his chocolate bar, ate another, and a whole box of Fig Newtons. Then he drank from the mountain stream and curled up beside the sleeping dragon.

Luckily, they didn't know who had seen them over Seaweed City. Ever since Mr. Wagonwheel had glimpsed the dragon Thursday he had been trying to persuade his neighbors that he really had seen a Blue Demon. No one believed a word of his story, but he had bothered the whole town so much that they told him to report it to the Seaweed City police. He had planned to go on Sunday, but changed his mind in the middle of Saturday night. He woke Mrs. Wagonwheel. "You take care of the morning milking, and I'll be back in time for dinner. I'm taking the horse and wagon."

"But..." said Mrs. Wagonwheel.

"I'm off!" said Mr. Wagonwheel, and Mrs. Wagonwheel heard the kitchen door slam behind him.

So, at dawn, just as he was trotting through the outskirts of Seaweed City, Mr. Wagonwheel looked up into the sky to see what sort of a day it was going to be. And he nearly fell out of his seat.

"The Blue Demon!" he screamed. "With a boy or something riding on its back!" He looked around wildly for someone to show it to, but nobody was in sight. And by the time he reached the police station and had found someone to listen to him, Elmer and the dragon were safely hidden in the forests of Spiky Mountain Range.

Chapter Nine

BLUELAND

Elmer and the dragon dozed on until late afternoon. They were both impatient to be off, but as Elmer said, "We'd only spoil everything by getting there before it's dark enough."

So they waited and rested and drank cool mountain water. The dragon munched ferns while Elmer ate his third chocolate bar.

"I can't stand it any longer," said the dragon,

jumping up and shaking out his wings.

"All right," said Elmer. "Let's go!" He put on his knapsack and climbed onto the dragon's back. They walked to a clearing in the woods, and the dragon took off across Awful Desert.

It was hot over the sands even in the late afternoon, and Elmer crouched over to hide from the burning winds. The dragon panted for air, but flew faster and faster, hardly daring to think what might have happened since he left. He kept muttering, "If only the sandstorms would start up! Where are the sandstorms? That would make the men leave us alone."

When they came to the dry rocky slopes of Blueland the sun was low on the horizon, and they knew it would soon be dark inside the circle of mountains.

"Keep a sharp lookout," warned the dragon as they picked their way through the boulders. "They may have men most anywhere."

Up, up they went, slowly, quietly. At last they

reached the gap between the peaks and Elmer gasped at the sight below him. The beautiful meadows of Blueland shone bright green, dotted with patches of snapdragons glowing white in the dimming light. And at the center the lake water reflected the pink of the sky. Suddenly it was gone into darkness as the sun set.

But the dragon had been straining to see across the lake and suddenly he grabbed Elmer for joy. "The men, I saw the men, and they were still standing outside the cave with the net. Maybe we're not too late!"

He hurried Elmer down to the giant snapdragon bush which hid the entrance to the little tunnel. "I don't think they found it," he whispered happily as he pulled aside the roots and rocks.

"Neither do I," agreed Elmer, looking all around to be sure he'd remember the spot. Then he took off his knapsack and unpacked one whistle, one horn, the flashlight and the ball of string.

"Lower your neck so I can measure the strings for

your whistle and horn," he said, getting out his jack-knife.

"Why do I have to have them on strings?" asked the dragon.

"I don't want you to drop them. If the men never see them, maybe they'll never guess what happened."

The dragon laughed, and tried out the strings to make sure he could reach the horn and whistle easily. "They're fine," he said. "Now I'll wait here until you tell me it's time. Look, the men are building a campfire. They must be having supper."

"So much the better," said Elmer as he started down into the tunnel with his knapsack. "But how will your family know I'm your friend?"

"Tell them Boris sent you."

"Boris! Is that your name?"

"Yes," said Boris uncomfortably. "I was embarrassed to tell you before."

"It's no worse than Elmer," said Elmer.

223

"I suppose not, and it's certainly not so bad as some in my family. I might as well tell you the rest. My sisters are Ingeborg, Eustacia, Gertrude, Bertha, Mildred and Hildegarde. And my brothers are Emil, Horatio, Conrad, Jerome, Wilhelm, Dagobert and Egmont. Can you imagine! But hurry! I can't wait to hear what's been happening to them all."

Once inside the tunnel Elmer snapped on his flashlight and shot it over the damp walls. The ceiling was high enough so he could walk easily. Down, down he went, around curves, through small rooms and then more narrow tunnels until at last he came to the place

where the dragon had got stuck. He heard scratching and scraping noises and he knew he must be very
close to the dragon family.

"It's Elmer Elevator, Boris's friend," he whispered
as bravely as he could.

"Who?"

"Elmer Elevator, Boris's friend. Boris is out at the entrance to the tunnel, and I've come to rescue you."

"Turn off your light and come in," whispered another voice, and Elmer walked slowly into the darkness. He stopped, and felt himself surrounded by huge forms breathing excitedly.

"We can't tell you how grateful we are," said the gigantic dragon mother.

"Never mind that," whispered the father. "What's your plan and how can we help? We're almost starved to death."

"Oh, have some chocolate bars," said Elmer, generously giving away his last three. "Here, I'll open them up for you, and divide each one into five pieces. I'm afraid it's not much, but it ought to help a little." He held his flashlight inside the knapsack and divided up the chocolate as he explained his plan. They all chuckled low dragon chuckles and began to feel much better.

Then Elmer made string necklaces for horns and whistles for all the dragons and carefully tied them on. He wanted to take a really good look at the tremendous family, but they were near the entrance to the cave and he had to keep the flashlight in the knapsack. As he took out his cap pistol he asked, "Do you know how heavy the net is, and how it's fastened across the entrance?"

"No," answered the dragon father.

"Well, I'd better look," said Elmer. He quietly crept up toward the net, but the men were sitting close by and he didn't dare get near enough to see it well.

"We'll have to trust to luck," he told the dragons as he started back through the tunnel to Boris.

Chapter Ten

ESCAPE

"Boris! Boris!" whispered Elmer from under the snapdragon bush.

"Are they all right? What's happened?"

"Nothing's happened. Everyone's all right, and we're ready to go. I couldn't see the net, but we'll hope for the best. Did you say one of the men is called Frank?"

"Yes. I heard them mention a Frank and an Albert."

"Good. I'll meet you here afterwards. I told your family you'd have to take me back and that you'd find them near here someplace."

"Fine," said the dragon. "I can't wait."

"All right, now. I'm going back. Remember, as soon as you hear my cap pistol the third time, you're to make as much noise with the horn and whistle as you possibly can."

Elmer turned back down into the tunnel and hurried to the big cave. Everyone was ready. "Boris will be your signal," he explained. "As soon as you hear him blowing his horn and whistle, you're all to blow as hard as you can in every direction. I'll yell 'Boris' when it's time to charge, but look carefully at the net before you try to pass by. I don't know where the opening will be. Ready?" whispered Elmer, his heart pounding so hard he was sure it must echo through the cave.

"Ready!" whispered the fifteen waiting dragons.

Elmer crept up close to the net. The men were unrolling blankets and getting ready for the night. There was no moon.

"Perfect!" thought Elmer. He took out his cap pistol and fired it once. Then, "Help! Help!" he cried in a gruff voice. "Get me out of here. I'm trapped!"

The men jumped up, tripping all over their blankets and bumping into one another.

"What was that?"

"Somebody's in the cave!"

"Frank, Albert, help, help!" yelled Elmer again.

"Come on, let's hurry," said the men and they began moving great boulders off the edge of the net.

"So that's how they fastened down the bottom," thought Elmer. "That should make it easy." Then he shot off his pistol again, and cried, "They got me! Help!"

The men frantically rolled away the boulders. Just as they began pulling aside the heavy net, Elmer shot off the pistol for the third time and ran back into the cave.

Boris heard the third shot and began blowing his whistle and horn and running up and down over the meadow. As the noise echoed over the lake the fifteen trapped dragons started in on their whistles and horns.

Noise roared wildly through the cave, back and forth across the lake, and echoed madly around the circle of mountains.

Some of the men had started off when they heard Boris; the others who had been about to rescue Elmer ran out of the cave in terror.

Elmer shouted "Boris!" and raced back through the tunnel.

The fifteen dragons surged toward the entrance, found where the men had pulled aside the net and poured through the opening, trampling out the campfire as they came. Into the sky they zoomed, still blowing their whistles and horns. Then they disappeared

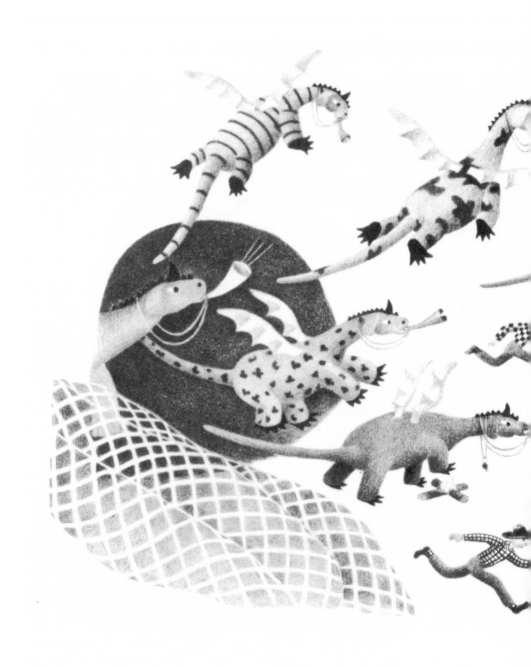

into the darkness, leaving thirteen men scattered over the meadows where they had fled, and three men sitting in the lake water where they had jumped.

"What happened?" said Frank to Albert.

Chapter Eleven

"THE DRAGON AFFAIR"

Elmer ran up to the tunnel to Boris and away they flew long before the noise had stopped echoing among the mountains.

"Well, that's that!" said Elmer, panting for breath and reaching for his second box of Fig Newtons.

"Gosh, Elmer, I can't thank you enough!" said the dragon.

"Never mind that. I never had so much fun in my life. But you'll have to hurry me back to Seaweed City. I've got to take the train home as fast as possible."

Over the desert they flew, and the wind grew stronger and stung Elmer's face.

"I think a storm's coming up," said the dragon. "I

can smell the sand in the air."

"Wonderful!" cried Elmer. "The men will have to leave Blueland, and maybe you'll never be bothered again."

Over Spiky Mountain Range they sped, reaching the outskirts of Seaweed City at midnight.

"How about leaving you on top of the monument?" suggested the dragon. "Then I won't have to land on the ground."

"Fine," said Elmer, and the dragon glided onto the top of Seaweed City Monument overlooking the center of the city.

"Goodbye for the last time," said Elmer. "I'm sorry that I never really got to see your family. They must be magnificent! But tell them from me that nobody will ever know more about them than they do right now, except for our friend the old alley cat. I'll tell her all about it."

"Goodbye! I'd better hurry home, too," sobbed the

happy baby dragon. He clumsily hugged Elmer, and off he flew.

Elmer finished up the Fig Newtons, saving one box for the train, and climbed down the monument. Quickly he walked to the railroad station and asked for a ticket to Nevergreen City.

"Isn't it rather late for a boy of your size to be taking the train alone?" asked the ticket agent.

"I suppose so," answered Elmer, giving the man $7.27.

The man shrugged his shoulders and handed Elmer a ticket. "I can't get used to boys these days," he muttered. "By the way, there's a train in twenty minutes. Gets you down in Nevergreen at noon."

"Thanks," said Elmer, jingling the nine cents he had left in his pocket as if he were used to taking trains in the middle of the night.

When the train thundered into the station Elmer climbed aboard. "What are you doing, running away from home?" asked the conductor suspiciously.

"Oh, no sir. On the contrary, I'm on my way there now," said Elmer, looking the conductor straight in the eye.

"Have it your own way," said the conductor, punching the ticket.

Elmer slept right through to Nevergreen City. He walked up the front steps of his home just as his mother was making herself some lunch. "Elmer, Elmer, you're back! But you look half-starved!"

"I am!" said Elmer, hugging his mother and sitting down at the table. He ate three bowls of tomato soup, five slices of pumpernickel bread, four glasses of milk, six fried eggs, and two huge pieces of sponge cake. Then he went to talk to the cat.

It wasn't until the next morning that the "dragon affair" came out in the "Nevergreen City News."

"Listen to this!" yelled Mr. Elevator, reading aloud at breakfast: " 'A fantastic and unexplainable escape took place in the great, high mountains of Blueland late Sunday night. Fifteen dragons, a wonder in themselves as they have long been believed extinct...' " and the newspaper story went on to tell about the brave men who had fought their way back through treacherous sandstorms to tell "the most momentous story of our time."

" 'Unbelievers who doubt this story,' " continued Mr.

Elevator, reading aloud from the paper, " 'will find it difficult to dismiss the following supporting evidence of the presence of dragons in this region.' " Then he proceeded to read about a ship stationed off the coast of Popsicornia which twice had sighted a strange flying beast, once with a boy atop it. And about a certain Mr. Wagonwheel who claimed also to have seen it twice, once on the ground near his farm, and once in the air with a boy aboard, over Seaweed City. And about Chester DeWitt, a small boy who also claimed he'd seen the dragon over the city the preceding Thursday evening. Lastly, there was a short bit about the conductor and the ticket agent, who wondered if the boy they had seen late Sunday night could have had anything to do with the case, and so on.

Mr. Elevator dropped the paper and stared at Elmer. "Did you have anything to do with all this? I just don't understand your strange trips away from home."

"Me?" said Elmer, choking on a piece of toast. "Why, Father, you don't mean you really believe all that nonsense, do you?"

THE END

BLUELAND

Bushes

Men on Slope

AWFUL DESERT